The
Secret Language

By URSULA NORDSTROM

Illustrated by Meg Wohlberg

SCHOLASTIC BOOK SERVICES

NEW YORK • TORONTO • LONDON • AUCKLAND • SYDNEY

FOR *Charlotte*

CONTENTS

New Girl

Sooner or later everyone has to go away from home for the first time. Sometimes it happens when a person is young. Sometimes it happens when a person is old. But sooner or later it does happen to everyone. It happened to Victoria North when she was eight.

The other children in the Coburn Home School bus shouted at one another, and pushed one another, and ran up and down the aisle. But Victoria sat alone looking out the window.

The bus turned down a country road, and suddenly one of the boys cried, "There's the old dump!"

"Coburn School! Coburn Home School!" the bus driver called. "All out!"

A pale, bony girl stood waiting for the bus. "Victoria North!" she yelled. "Victoria North, Victoria North, Victoria Victoria North North! I'm looking for a new girl named Victoria North! Any new kids on this bus?" She looked at Victoria. "That you? Well, I'm your roommate. My name is Ann Spear. Come on and I'll show you our room." She walked toward a large brick building and Victoria followed her. Yellow leaves lay across the graveled path, and in the distance the hills were blue with mist.

"This is the girls' dormitory," Ann said as she opened the front door. "It's called Wingate Hall. The boys live in Shippen Hall. Do you like boys?"

Victoria looked at Ann. She was too homesick to speak.

"Well, I don't," Ann said flatly and started up a flight of stairs. "But we just see them in classes. We have separate dining rooms. I've been here for two years and I'm supposed to tell you about everything. Anyhow, the boys at this school are all awful, if you ask me."

At the head of the stairs Ann turned and led Victoria down a long hall. "This is our corridor," Ann said. "Our housemother is Miss Mossman, and she is very very very strict." She opened a door. "Here's our room."

Victoria's trunk, which someone had unlocked for her, stood next to one of the beds.

"You'd better unpack now," Ann said. "I'm going back down to see what other old girls came back. See you later."

Victoria hung her hat and coat in the closet and slowly unpacked her trunk. On every article of clothing her mother had sewn a name tape, in accordance with the instructions in the Coburn Home School catalogue. At home, Victoria had liked the way her name looked woven in red on the white tape. But now, in this new place, the name tapes made even her most familiar possessions seem strange to her.

When she hung up her flannel bathrobe, she found a note from her mother pinned to it. In the note her mother asked her to remember to wear clean underwear every day and to say her prayers every night. And then her mother said Christmas vacation would come soon. The note made Victoria more homesick than she had been before. After she put on her new dark-blue dress, she stood looking out the window, trying not to cry.

Ann came back in a little while. She looked at Victoria critically. "What's the matter with your *collar?*" she said impatiently. "My goodness, it's all twisted. Here, I'll fix it. My goodness, you can't even dress yourself yet!" Ann frowned as she pulled Victoria's collar straight.

There was a heavy knock at the door, and a tall woman came in. "How do you do, Victoria?" she said. "I am your housemother, Miss Mossman." Miss Mossman was an ugly woman, with straight black hair and little black eyes. "I'm glad to have you on my corridor," she said. "Ann will explain our rules and regulations to you, and I am sure you will find them easy to obey. I will see you at my table at supper."

Miss Mossman left, and Victoria sat down on her bed.

"We are not allowed to sit on the beds," Ann said sharply. "Sit on your chair. My goodness!"

Victoria went over to the window and carefully wrapped the cord of the shade around her thumb. She was trying not to cry in front of Ann.

In a few minutes a gong sounded, and Ann jumped up. "Come on," she said. "Supper! Hurry up!"

In the dining room, Victoria followed Ann to one of the long tables and sat down next to her.

"Oh, you don't sit here, dopey," Ann said. "You're supposed to sit at Miss Mossman's table. She told you!"

Victoria stumbled to her feet. She didn't know which table was Miss Mossman's, and in the blur of strange faces she couldn't find the housemother. All the other children were at their places. At the sound of a bell all heads were lowered and grace was said aloud. "For what we are about to receive may the good Lord make us truly thankful." The words echoed around Victoria as she stood alone in the middle of the dining room. When grace was over, Victoria saw Miss Mossman beckoning to her.

"Girls," Miss Mossman said, "this is Victoria North, a new student this year. Victoria, there's your place, between Sue Burton and Eleanor Mindendorfer." She briefly introduced the other girls. Several of them looked up and said "Hi" as Victoria slid into her seat and stared at the plate of food in front of her. Sue Burton, who was fat and had red hair, said, "What's your name again?"

But Victoria didn't hear her.

"Please pass the bread," said Eleanor Mindendorfer loudly.

"How come you came back, Martha?" Sue said to a dark girl with bangs who sat opposite Victoria. "I thought you weren't coming back this year."

The dark girl scowled. "I'm probably only going to stay until Thanksgiving," she said.

"But I thought you weren't coming back at all this year," Sue insisted. "You did say you were going to live home. I remember. But I was sure you'd have to come back anyhow, though."

"M.Y.O.D.O.B. And that means Mind Your Own Dumb Old Business," Martha said clearly.

"Martha!" Miss Mossman said. "There is no need to be rude to Sue. Why, Victoria, you're not eating your supper. Here at Coburn School we eat what is placed in front of us, Victoria. Come, dear."

Victoria picked up her fork and tried to swallow some food.

"My little brother is coming to this school next year, Miss Mossman," Eleanor Mindendorfer announced.

"That's splendid, Eleanor. What is his name?"

"His name is Sidney, and he's my little brother, and — "

"Oh, ick-en-spick," Martha said.

"What?" Eleanor looked at her. "What did you say, Martha?"

"I said ick-en-spick," Martha repeated.

"Oh, Martha, you're so funny!" Eleanor began to giggle.

But Sue was indignant. "What kind of talk is that?" she asked. "It's crazy."

"Well, it isn't crazy."

"It certainly sounds crazy, if you ask me," Sue said.

"I didn't ask you, and it isn't crazy. Neither is 'ankendosh.' Neither is 'leebossa.'"

"Martha Sherman, what are you talking about?" Sue was puzzled.

"I'm talking about a secret language I just happen to know."

"What do you mean? What secret language?"

"It's just my secret language, that's all," Martha said.

"What was that funny word you said?"

"Ick-en-spick."

"What does it mean? And what did that other funny word you said mean?"

"Wouldn't you like to know?" said Martha, and she made a hideous face at Sue.

"Now, Martha," said Miss Mossman from the head of the table. "You must stop being rude. Stop it at once."

"She's a big fat dope," Martha said.

"Martha! You must behave yourself, or I will have to ask you to leave the table. Eleanor, I know you must be looking forward to having your little brother here next year."

"Yes, I am, Miss Mossman. He is a year and two months younger than I am, and his name is Sidney, and — "

"Well, what's so wonderful about that?" Martha asked.

"Well! I guess I can talk about my brother if I want to!"

"Oh, all right. Tell some more. Go ahead." Martha shrugged. "His name is Sidney, and he's coming to this school next year."

"Yes, he is," Eleanor said.

"Poor old Sidney," said Martha heavily.

Everyone turned to look at the housemother. Two bright-red spots appeared on Miss Mossman's cheeks, and her right eye began to twitch. She said sternly, "Martha, you may go to your room at once. Although you have been back at Coburn less than one day, I will have to give you a demerit. Now go to your room immediately. I'll talk to you later."

Martha folded her napkin, pushed back her chair, and left the dining room slowly. She was still scowling.

"She's an awful girl," Sue said to the rest of the table. "She's the worst girl in this whole school."

"That will be enough, Susan," Miss Mossman said severely.

"I think she is the worst girl here," Sue whispered to Victoria. "Some people in this school think she is so wonderful, and she thinks she is too, but I think she is awful."

Victoria didn't answer.

"Victoria, you haven't touched your food," Miss Mossman said. "Now finish your supper at once."

Victoria stared at her plate.

"Victoria, did you hear me? Eat your supper at once. The rest of us are waiting for you."

Tears suddenly spilled over Victoria's cheeks. They ran down her face and fell on her clasped hands. She lowered her head. Everyone at the table looked at her.

"Victoria," Miss Mossman said sharply. "Look at me, Victoria."

Slowly Victoria turned toward the head of the table. With her eyes shut and her mouth twisted, she wept soundlessly. Several of the girls began to giggle.

Miss Mossman saw that Victoria was indeed unable to eat. "You may clear," she said to the maid.

After supper the children sat on folding chairs in the drawing room for an hour of singing.

"Turn, please, to page eighty-seven. 'A Capital Ship,'" Miss Mossman said as Miss Douglass sat down at the piano.

"A Capital Ship" was a gay song, and everyone loved it.

Next Miss Mossman announced, "Page forty-one. 'Now the Day Is Over.'"

To Victoria, sitting in the front row next to Ann, the slow music and the words,

"Now the day is over,
  Night is drawing nigh,
  Shadows of the evening steal across the sky"

seemed the saddest she had ever heard. In the middle
of the song she started again to cry.

"Oh, stop it!" Ann whispered. "Stop crying!" And
she shook the songbook in exasperation.

The next song was "The Harp That Once Through
Tara's Halls." It, too, was a sad song, and Victoria continued to cry. Finally Miss Mossman motioned to Ann
to take Victoria out. Behind her disgusted and resentful
roommate, Victoria stumbled slowly from the room.

Upstairs Ann stood with her hands on her hips and
glared at Victoria. "You're an awful crybaby," Ann said.
She picked up her towel and washcloth and flounced
out of the room.

Victoria pulled off her dress and her shoes, and got
into bed in her underwear and socks. She was shivering,
though it was not a cold night. She did not even think of
saying her prayers.

Ann came back. "Aren't you going to get washed?"
she asked.

Victoria was crying, and she couldn't answer.

"Are you just going to leave your dress on the floor?"
There was no answer.

"You'll get a demerit," Ann said spitefully. "Don't say
I didn't tell you. Miss Mossman may even give you two
demerits. I don't care, though."

The singing was over. Girls came upstairs noisily to get ready for bed. They shouted to each other in the corridor, banged doors, ran back and forth to the bathrooms. Suddenly there was a loud blast on a whistle, and then there was silence. Ann snapped out the light and got into bed.

Victoria tried to be quiet. But she was crying so hard that she had to gasp when she tried to catch her breath. Every time Victoria did that, Ann turned over noisily in bed and heaved an irritated sigh. Finally Ann sat up and whispered crossly, "Oh, stop *bawling!*" Then she flopped back down in her bed and sighed loudly again. After awhile Ann went to sleep.

This was the first night Victoria had ever spent away from her mother, and it was worse than the worst nightmare she had ever had. Her mother couldn't have known it would be like this! Gasping and choking, Victoria rolled over on her back, stared up into the dark, and wept. The tears rolled down her cheeks into her ears, and she turned over on her side and wiped her face and her ears on the stiff sheet. Today had been as awful as anything could be, and she had lived through it. She had lived through today, but what about tomorrow? What would she do tomorrow?

Finally, sobbing and gasping, she grew tired. After a long time, she turned over once more and put her head under the pillow. And then at last she fell asleep, too.

The Secret Language

"WAKE UP!" Ann cried. She shook Victoria's shoulder, "The whistle just blew. Hurry up for inspection!"

Victoria pulled on her bathrobe and hurried into the hall behind her roommate. At the end of the corridor the housemother stood waiting to see that everyone was out of bed. When all the girls were lined up two by two in front of their doors, Miss Mossman called, "Dismissed!" and blew the whistle again.

"Breakfast in half an hour!" Ann yelled, and ran down the hall to the bathroom. Victoria followed her slowly.

"My, your eyes are all red," Sue Burton remarked, looking at Victoria in the mirror over the washbasins. "I guess you cry an awful lot. Don't you like it here?"

Victoria shook her head and bent over a basin. Sue began to talk across her to Ann. "Miss Mossman is just as mean as ever, with all those whistles and morning inspection and everything," Sue said.

"Yes." Ann sighed. "That standing in the hall gives

me a pain. She must have been a jail mother before, not a housemother."

Victoria finished brushing her teeth, and as she straightened up, Sue and Ann both looked at her and giggled. Several other girls did too. Suddenly Martha, the girl who had been dismissed from the table the night before came in, dragging a towel. "What's so funny?" she asked.

"I guess that new girl's homesick," Sue said. "She was crying during singing last night, and Ann had to take her out, and her face looks funny."

"Oh, ankendosh," Martha said. "How old are you, anyhow?" she said to Victoria.

Martha sounded friendly, but Victoria hurried past her without speaking and went back to her room to get dressed.

The day wore on. Victoria went to the school hall with Ann and the others, and met the teachers. No class-work was done, but books were distributed and desks were assigned.

After the last class was dismissed, Victoria walked out of the school hall behind Ann, who was whispering and giggling with Eleanor Mindendorfer. As they went out the door, Ann turned to Victoria and said crossly, "Oh, hang off me, will you? You've been hanging on me all day! Just please hang off me!" Then Ann walked away with Eleanor and some of the other old girls.

Victoria stood by the school hall and looked around

her. She didn't know where to go or what to do. In a few minutes Miss Blanchard, the arithmetic teacher, came out the door. "Hello," she said. "You're Victoria North, aren't you? I think Victoria is a pretty name."

Victoria looked up at her, but could think of nothing to say.

"Why don't you go down to the swings for a while? That will be fun. In a few days you will know more of the other children and you'll be happier, Victoria. Really you will be. I know it is hard at first."

Victoria was silent, and finally Miss Blanchard turned and walked away. Victoria picked up some gravel and looked at it carefully, then let it fall slowly out of her hand. She examined the bark on a tree for a few minutes. Then she walked back to her room.

The first ten days at Coburn Home School were all lonely ones for Victoria. She didn't know anyone, and no one seemed to want to know her. Her mother wrote her every day, but the letters only made Victoria more homesick.

Then one afternoon, late in September, Victoria was alone down by the swings. Martha wandered by and saw her. "Hello," she said. She sat on the end of a slide. "That's some dumb table we're at," she added. "I wish I could be at Miss Blanchard's table."

Victoria was afraid to say something Martha might think was silly. So she said nothing. But she smiled.

"I hate this old school," Martha said.

"Oh, so do I!" Victoria said.

"I hate it," Martha repeated. "And it's worse than it was last year. But I only came back for a little while, anyhow. Pretty soon I'm going to live home and go to day school. Are you going home for Thanksgiving?"

Victoria shook her head. "I guess not."

"Well I am, and I just bet I won't have to come back here. I'm going to tell my mother and father about this school. I'll tell them about the food. I'll tell them they give us horrible, disgusting, dirty, gluey purple stuff to eat and they call it oatmeal."

Victoria was startled but fascinated.

"Does your family live in New York?" Martha asked.

"My mother does, most of the time."

"What do you mean, most of the time?"

"Well, she has to go away once in awhile. She works. That's why I can't go home for Thanksgiving."

"Where's she going?"

"Chicago."

"My father's an importer. What's yours?"

Victoria could hardly remember him. "I haven't any," she said.

"You just have a mother?"

"Yes."

"Oh. Lots of the kids here just have a mother, too. Or just a father. What's your favorite subject?"

"Reading. What's yours?"

"Arithmetic."

"Arithmetic!" Victoria was amazed. "Oh, I hate arithmetic!"

"Well, I hate reading," Martha said reasonably. "What are you going to be when you grow up?"

"I don't know yet. What are you?"

"Oh, I guess I'll be an inventor, or maybe a singer. Oh, I certainly hate this school," Martha repeated. "I hate all the buildings and all the rooms and the food, and I even hate the swings, and I hate this dumb slide." She kicked the slide as she spoke.

"It's an awful old school," Victoria agreed. And she gave the slide a little kick too.

Suddenly Martha stood up and marched around one of the swings with her stomach stuck out in what seemed to Victoria an extremely amusing way. Then Martha sang in a piercing voice:

> "Two more months to vacation.
>   Then I go to the station.
>   Back to civilization.
>   Back to Mother and home."

"Did you make that up?" Victoria asked, impressed.

"Me? No! You never heard that before? I guess that's

just because you never went to boarding school before. I can make up stuff, though, if I want to."

Victoria thought Martha was wonderful. They climbed up on a seesaw, and seesawed up and down in the darkening light. Then they went to the dormitory to get ready for dinner.

At the table that night Martha looked across at Victoria and said, "Hey, Vick, maybe we'll have ice cream tonight. That would be leebossa, wouldn't it?"

The other girls looked at Martha in surprise, and then at Victoria.

"Wouldn't it? Wouldn't it be leebossa?" Martha repeated, staring at Victoria.

"Yes, I guess so," Victoria said finally.

"After singing, I'll tell you all about my secret language," Martha said. "But you'll have to promise you'll never tell anyone else!"

"I promise," said Victoria faintly.

The other girls looked at Victoria with new interest. Martha had never been so friendly with anyone else.

That night, when singing was over, Martha waited in the hall for Victoria and they walked upstairs together.

" 'Ick-en-spick' is for when something is silly," Martha explained. "Or like when someone is trying to get in good with a teacher and is trying to be very sweet. You know. Goody-goody stuff is ick-en-spick."

Victoria nodded.

" 'Ankendosh,' " Martha went on, "is for something

mean or disgusting. Ann Spear is usually very anken-dosh."

"She certainly is," Victoria said.

"Now, 'leebossa' is for when you like something. When something is just lovely or when something works out just right, it is leebossa. For anything especially nice you can say 'leeleeleeleebossa.' But that's only for something really wonderful. Understand?"

"Yes, thank you for telling me. Are there any other words?"

"No. But maybe we can make up some more," Martha said.

"That would be leebossa," Victoria said, and Martha grinned at her.

From then on Martha and Victoria were friends. Whenever possible, they did their homework with each other. They walked to and from the school hall together every day. And they sat next to each other at singing every night.

Being friends with Martha was wonderful, and Victoria was happier than she had been. But she was still afraid of Miss Mossman, and she still missed her mother, and she still counted the days to Christmas vacation.

Ann Spear Goes Home

SLOWLY VICTORIA began to like some things about boarding school. But Martha didn't. Martha said every day that she was not coming back to Coburn School the next year. Victoria knew she would have to, and she wanted Martha to come back too.

"Not me," said Martha firmly. "I'm going to stay home and go to day school. And I won't have any old whistles blowing at me all the time. And I won't have to stand in the corridor for inspection and freeze every morning. I'm just going to live home and go to day school, and I'll even go home every day for lunch."

"Wouldn't that be leebossa!" Victoria sighed. "My mother can't have me live with her just because she has to go to work. Otherwise I'd live at home. My mother really wants me to."

"Well, so does my mother, and my father too," Martha said. "But they said they think I'll learn more at boarding school than I would at day school. They said so."

23

"Sue Burton told me her mother told her that boarding school would probably help her learn to get along with other people," Victoria said slowly. "Isn't that funny?"

"It sure is," Martha said. "Nobody could ever get along with that dopey Sue Burton at boarding school or day school or any school. Well, anyhow, next year I am going to day school, and I will go home every single day for lunch."

That was what many of the children longed to do. Even those who liked Coburn School often talked of the time when they could live at home and go to day school.

And when it finally happened to one of them, it happened to Ann Spear. It was unbelievable, Victoria thought, that such a wonderful thing could happen to a mean girl like Ann Spear. But it did.

"Every day I'll go home right after school," Ann boasted. "And I'm going to have ice cream and cake any time I want. And my mother will let me keep my light on at night as long as I want to."

"You'll have to start school in the middle of the term," Martha interrupted. "You'll be a new girl."

As soon as Martha said it, she was sorry. So she added, "But, oh boy, you're lucky. Just think, you won't have to eat any of that old oatmeal!"

Ann nodded happily. "Maybe you can live home next year," she said, suddenly trying to be pleasant.

"Oh, I'm not coming back here next year," Martha

said. "No maybe about it, I wouldn't come back here for eight million dollars, and I know my mother and father won't make me. But, anyhow, as long as Ann is leaving — " and Martha turned to Victoria — "let's us get permission to room together."

"Oh, Martha, do you think they'd let us!"

"I'll ask Miss Mossman today," Martha said. "I don't see why not. Ruth Harkins doesn't want to room with me any more than I want to room with her. I'll ask Miss Mossman."

The housemother didn't say yes immediately. But she did say she would think about it and would discuss it with Mrs. Coburn. Two days before Ann was to leave, Miss Mossman called Martha and Victoria into her office after breakfast.

"We have decided to let you girls room together," Miss Mossman said. "Martha, you will move into Victoria's room Saturday morning, after Ann leaves."

"Thank you very much, Miss Mossman," said Martha.

"Thank you very much, Miss Mossman," said Victoria.

"Now, girls, I must tell you that I was against this move. I think you should both try to make other friends. But Mrs. Coburn is willing to give you girls an opportunity to behave yourselves and to obey the rules. Do you promise to behave, Martha?"

"Yes, I do," Martha said.

"And you, Victoria?"

"Yes, I do," said Victoria.

"Very well. You may go."

Outside Miss Mossman's office they looked at each other and smiled. Then Victoria said, "Very leebossa."

As always, Martha was direct and intent about what she was going to do. Thursday evening she came to Victoria's room with some pajamas and underwear, and asked Ann Spear to let her put them in one of her bureau drawers.

Ann was furious. "You get out of here, you old Martha Sherman," Ann said. "I'm not going until Saturday. I'm not even packed yet! My goodness!"

The next night, about ten minutes after lights-out, Victoria heard the door of the room open quietly. She sat up in bed and saw Martha standing in the doorway.

Victoria was horrified. Miss Mossman's most strictly enforced rule was that no girl was to go to another girl's room after lights-out. Victoria was too frightened to speak. Martha slowly closed the door and stood still, trying to get her bearings in the dark room.

"Hey, Vicky," she said softly.

"Oh, Martha! If she ever catches you!" Victoria said in a terrified whisper.

"She won't catch me," Martha whispered back.

"Martha, she'll give you a million demerits! She won't let us room together!"

"She won't catch me," Martha repeated in a whisper. "I had a good idea I have to tell you!"

Ann Spear, suddenly wakened out of a sound sleep, sat up. "The what? Tell who? What's that?" Ann spoke in a loud, clear voice.

"Sssssssssssssh!"

Martha dived into the closet and closed the door. Victoria lay down and shut her eyes.

"Victoria, that was Martha!" Ann whispered, now thoroughly awake.

"Ann, please don't talk! Miss Mossman will come in!" Victoria was frightened. "Please don't talk, Ann!"

And then they heard Miss Mossman walking rapidly down the hall. There was a knock on their door, and Miss Mossman came in. "What was the meaning of that noise?" She snapped on the overhead light.

Victoria sat up and blinked, as though she had been asleep. She simply could not let Miss Mossman discover Martha in the closet. "What, Miss Mossman?" Victoria asked sleepily.

"Victoria, I distinctly heard some noise from this room. Now, what was it?"

Victoria lay down again and looked helplessly at Miss Mossman. Then Ann turned over noisily in her bed and looked up. "Why, Miss Mossman," Ann said, and sat up. "I didn't hear anything. I was asleep!"

The housemother looked from one to the other. "Now, I don't want to hear any more noise from this room, and I mean that," she said. She snapped off the light and went out.

Several minutes passed, and then slowly the closet door opened and Martha tiptoed out. She stood in the middle of the room and whispered, "Thanks, Ann."

"You get out, Martha Sherman," Ann whispered furiously. "You get out and stay out. I should have told her to look in the closet. Now, get out!"

"All right, all right. I just wanted to talk to Vicky, but all right. I'll leave. Anyhow, Ann, I'm glad I never made a pie bed on you."

Martha tiptoed to the door, opened it silently, and went out.

Victoria lay still, her heart beating hard. Finally she said softly, "Thanks, Ann."

"Oh, be quiet," Ann muttered.

"Ann, what's a pie bed?" Victoria asked.

"My goodness, don't you even know what a pie bed is?" Ann whispered in her old sneering way.

"No, I don't. Please tell me."

"It's too hard to describe. And if we whisper any more, Miss Mossman will come back and kill us. My goodness, I thought everybody knew what a pie bed is."

"What's it like, Ann?"

"Oh, you'll find out, rooming with that Martha," Ann replied. "You'll probably find out very very very soon." Ann turned over and went to sleep.

Victoria stayed awake for a long time. Rooming with Martha was certainly going to be exciting, she thought. Finally she went to sleep, too.

Roommates

THE NEXT DAY Ann's parents drove out to the school to take their daughter home. Several children, including Martha and Victoria, stood silently on the steps and watched while Mr. Spear put Ann's suitcases in the car. Miss Mossman chatted with Mrs. Spear and Ann, who sat in the front seat. Then Mr. Spear got into the car and started the motor. Ann, sitting between her parents, leaned forward and waved. "Good-bye!" she cried.

"Good-bye, Ann dear!" called Miss Mossman. "Good-bye, Mr. and Mrs. Spear!" Miss Mossman waved, and a few of the children did too, and then the car rolled slowly down the driveway.

Martha turned to Victoria. "That old Miss Mossman always acts so sweet in front of parents," she said. "Come on, Vick. Now we can move my stuff in with yours."

Martha had the most interesting things Victoria had ever seen. She had a phonograph, a transistor radio, binoculars, and a Polaroid camera. Even her pencil box was unusually beautiful. It was dark-red leather, and her initials were stamped on the cover in gold. It had two drawers, one for crayons and one for pencils. There were separate compartments for rubber bands, paper clips, a pencil sharpener, and an eraser. Martha also had an especially fine flashlight. It had three different lights: white, red, and green.

"Oh, this is the best flashlight!" Victoria sighed, flicking it from red to green to white, and back to red again.

"You want it?" Martha said. "You can have it. I don't need it."

"Oh no, thanks, Martha," said Victoria, putting the flashlight down. "Thanks just the same. But I'll borrow it."

"Any time," Martha said, and shrugged. "My father'll get me another one anyhow."

When they were getting ready for bed that night, Martha said, "Vicky, do you like Miss Mossman at all?"

"Not much," Victoria admitted.

"She gets so cross so quick," Martha said. She sat down with her bedroom slippers in her hands and thought about the housemother. When Miss Mossman was cross, her right eye always twitched in a sort of wink. It wasn't a friendly wink, Martha thought. It was a rather terrifying wink, as she looked at you sternly and told you once more and for the last time to go to your room.

"I just wonder why she *winks* like that," Martha said. She went over to the mirror and stared at her reflection and began to talk like Miss Mossman. She even seemed to look like her. "Now, Martha Sherman," Martha said severely, looking at herself in the mirror and winking her right eye, "you march yourself right upstairs and get your room picked up before I count to ten." Martha frowned and winked angrily at herself in the mirror. "I'll give you a demerit. I'll give you two demerits. I'll give you — "

"Oh, Martha!" Victoria shook with laughter and horror. "What if she came in now! Oh, Martha, stop!"

"And that whistle!" Martha said, turning away from the mirror. "Why does she have to blow that old whistle all the time and make us form a line by two's? Miss Douglass doesn't run her corridor with an old whistle!"

"Maybe next year we can be in Miss Douglass' corridor," Victoria suggested.

"Not me. I'm not coming back next year," Martha reminded her quickly.

That night, after the lights-out whistle blew, they both sat cross-legged on Martha's bed and pulled a blanket over their heads. Victoria held Martha's flashlight, and she turned on the white light.

"Tell some more about before you came to this school," Martha said.

Victoria and her mother had almost always lived in a hotel, and Martha loved to hear about it. "Go on, tell some more about the hotel," Martha said, pulling the blanket tighter.

"All right. But, first, what's a pie bed? You said you were glad you never made a pie bed on Ann. What is it?"

"Oh. Well, couldn't I just show you sometime?"

"Oh, Martha! Please tell me!"

"Well, let's see. You take the top sheet off someone's bed and hide it. Someone you don't like. And then you pull the bottom of the other sheet up so it looks as though there are two sheets on the bed. You know. You don't leave the bottom of the sheet tucked in at the bottom of the bed. You fold it back up so that the sheet just goes halfway down the bed. Then, when you put the blankets back on and fold the sheet back, it looks as though there were two sheets on the bed, and the person you don't like gets in and then can't put her feet down. She has to get up and make her bed all over again, and she gets mad, and that's a pie bed. Did you really always live in hotels?"

"Well, last year we had an apartment for awhile," Victoria said, switching the flashlight to the red light. It turned their faces and hands dark red. "We ate at home then every night."

"Did your mother cook?"

Victoria nodded, trying to remember that apartment more clearly. "Yes, she cooked," Victoria said slowly. "And she read to me after dinner, and I remember one book was about some poor little French children after a

war, or during a war, or something." She stopped, trying to remember. "And sometimes my mother let me
wash and dry the silver all alone," she said.

"What's so wonderful about that?" Martha asked. "I
wouldn't want to wash a lot of old knives and forks."

"Oh, Martha, it was fun," Victoria said, suddenly re-
membering it all. "It really was. When she let me do
them alone I had a good game about the battlefield."
Dreamily she switched the flashlight to the green light.

"The what? What battlefield? You're crazy," Martha
said.

"No, it was fun. I'd go out to the kitchen and there'd
be all those dirty knives and forks and spoons." She
stared at Martha's green face for a moment. "And I'd
pretend I was a lovely nurse and the kitchen was a horrible battlefield. I'd pretend the battle was over, and the
knives and things were wounded soldiers, and I was a
kind nurse. And I had to take care of all the poor dirty
soldiers. I'd pick them up and bathe them, and get
them clean and cured and dry, and put them in clean
beds in the hospital. The hospital was where we kept the
silver. And I fixed those poor wounded soldiers up and
put them to bed."

"Some dopey game," Martha said, but she looked interested.

"It sounds dumb," Victoria admitted. "But it was
fun."

The next morning, when the whistle woke them, Martha and Victoria sat up and fumbled around for their bathrobes and slippers. It was dark at six-thirty in the morning, and it was cold too.

"Oh, I hate this inspection stuff most of all," Martha grumbled as they joined the other children shivering in the corridor.

Sue Burton appeared at her door, across the hall. "Hi," she said sleepily. "I bet Ann Spear doesn't have to get up like this today. I bet she doesn't have to stand in any old hall."

The rest of the children stopped talking for a moment and thought about Ann Spear. Then Miss Mossman blew the whistle to dismiss them, and they hurried to get dressed.

Butterflies
or Ballet Dancers?

At breakfast one morning Sue Burton announced that her mother was sending her a costume for the Halloween costume party.

"Do you know what you're going as?" she asked Martha.

"Not yet," Martha said. "Vicky and I will go as something together, won't we, Vicky?"

"What's it all about? What's it like, Sue?" Victoria asked.

"Oh, everyone comes in wonderful costumes, and the best ones get prizes. Last year I was a beautiful princess, and Joe was a pirate, and Ann Spear came as a witch, and Edith Scott came as a character in some book. What was that book again, Edith?"

"It was a story, not a whole book," Edith said. "I came as the poor little match girl."

"Oh, that's right," Sue said, nodding. "You looked awful."

"Sue!" Miss Mossman looked at her reprovingly. "I'm sure Edith looked very sweet."

"Vicky," Martha whispered, "we won't go as anything so dumb. Don't worry about it."

Victoria was surprised. The costumes had not sounded at all dumb to her. As a matter of fact, she wished she and Martha could go as beautiful princesses themselves. But she knew they couldn't copy Sue. However, she hoped they would be able to think of something lovely to wear to the party.

After breakfast, as she and Martha made their beds, Victoria brought up the subject of their costumes.

"Oh, it isn't for two weeks," Martha said. "We have plenty of time."

A week later Victoria spoke again about the party. Still Martha assured her that there was plenty of time left and told her not to worry.

"But Martha, we have to decide soon!" Victoria said. "We have to get our costumes somehow!"

"Oh, don't worry so much," Martha told her. "We'll think of something. And we can make our own costumes."

"How about going as butterflies, Marth?"

But Martha looked so disgusted that Victoria let the subject drop.

The next day Victoria suggested that they go as ballet dancers. But that idea did not interest Martha.

"We will not go in any dumb costumes," Martha told her. "I still don't know just what we'll go as, but we'll think of something good."

Victoria sighed. She was worried.

Finally one morning, only three days before the party, Martha said, "Well, I thought of something good for us to be at the party."

"Oh, what, Martha?"

"Eyeglasses," Martha said. She smiled happily.

"Eyeglasses!" Victoria was horrified. "Oh, Martha, you're awful!"

"What's awful? It's a leebossa idea, Vick. We'll make big round things, sort of like round kites, out of paper, and draw a big eye on each of them, and we can figure out a way to put a sort of stick between them for the part that goes over the nose, and we'll each — "

"Martha Sherman!" Victoria was furious. "That is a simply terrible idea! I won't go as half of some old eyeglasses for anything! I think you're awful. Why can't we go as something pretty?"

"Like some lovely butterflies, I suppose?" said Martha, scowling.

"Well, at least not something crazy like eyeglasses! Oh, Martha!"

"All right," Martha said, suddenly reasonable again. "We won't go as eyeglasses. I'll think up something else, something good."

"Well, I certainly hope so!" Victoria said.

"Now, don't worry, Vick, I'll think of something really good," Martha promised.

What she thought of was chocolate ice-cream cones.

"They'll be easy to make," she told Victoria in bed that night.

"Oh, Martha!" Vicky groaned.

"Now, wait, Vick. I figured it all out. I talked to that new handy man today, and he thinks it's a wonderful idea, and he says he has lots of heavy cardboard for the cones. I'll draw little crisscrosses on the cardboard, so it looks like ice-cream cone material. Then Mr. Hardy — that's his name — can wrap the cardboard around us in a cone shape, so that the wide part for the ice cream will come just above our heads, and the point part will come down at our feet. Mr. Hardy can put some pieces of wire through the cardboard so it will stay in the cone shape. Then we'll get a lot of soft brown paper, tissue paper or something, to wad up and pile up inside the cones to look like chocolate ice cream! It will be leebossa, Vick!"

"Couldn't we be like those flat-bottomed cones?" Victoria asked faintly. "Then we could at least have our legs out."

"Oh, Vicky, that would be dumb! Anybody could do that. We have to be regular ice-cream cones."

"How will we walk?" Victoria asked.

"We'll leave enough room at the bottom of the cones so just our feet can come out. It will be wonderful, Vicky, honest. We'll be two great big enormous delicious leebossa chocolate ice-cream cones."

Then Martha went to sleep. But Victoria stayed awake for a long time. She was still worried.

The next day Mr. Hardy did help them make the cos-

tumes. Victoria still thought the idea was ridiculous, but she tried to act more cheerful about it than she felt. Her spirits lifted briefly when Mr. Hardy said he had no brown tissue paper for the chocolate ice cream.

"I have brown wrapping paper," he said thoughtfully. "But it's too heavy, and it wouldn't look anything like chocolate ice cream."

Martha was silent, and Victoria began to hope that they'd have to forget about going as chocolate ice-cream cones and go instead as something more simple, and perhaps even something pretty.

"I know," Martha said suddenly. "Mrs. Coburn has a lot of green tissue paper left over from that pageant last year. We can get some of that and go as *pistachio* ice-cream cones!"

"Oh, Martha!" wailed Victoria.

So they went as pistachio ice-cream cones. The space left for their feet was so small they could hardly walk. And they could hardly see because Mr. Hardy had made only the smallest slits in the cardboard for their eyes. And of course they couldn't eat any of the food at the party.

They hopped around slowly and peered at all the other children through the eye slits. When everyone else danced they stood silent and alone by the wall. Every once in a while some of the other children came and stood before them and stared at them curiously.

Finally it was time for the prizes to be awarded. Sue

Burton won the prize for the most beautiful costume. She was dressed as a Turkish lady. Joe Beall won the one for the best costume made by one of the students. He had come as Robin Hood. Then Mrs. Coburn said, "And now I'm sure we all agree that the prize for the most original costume should go to our two dear ice-cream cones."

There was a lot of applause, and Martha and Victoria hopped slowly forward. Mrs. Coburn placed the prize, which was a ribbon and a button with "Most Original" printed on it, in the green pistachio tissue-paper ice cream in Victoria's cone.

Victoria wanted to tell her that it should go to Martha because Martha had been the one to think of coming as ice-cream cones. But Victoria was too tired, and too hot and uncomfortable inside the cardboard cone, to know how to explain it.

That night in bed Martha sighed in contentment. "It was fun, wasn't it, Vicky?" she said happily.

"Yes," Victoria said. She was sleepy.

"We'll start earlier next year," Martha promised, "and we'll get a good idea again. I'll start thinking about it very soon. So don't worry."

"All right, Marth, I won't," Victoria murmured. But, sleepy as she was, suddenly she realized that Martha had apparently forgotten that she wasn't coming back next year.

And then they both fell asleep.

Ralmadil School

WHEN MARTHA came back to school after her Thanksgiving weekend in New York, she told Victoria all about it. Her parents had taken her iceskating, and to a matinee, and to the Music Hall. She had had a wonderful time.

"I told them all about this awful school," she said, "and they just want me to try to stand it until Christmas. So I said all right, I'd stay until Christmas."

"Oh, Marth! Really, won't you come back after Christmas? Oh, it will be awful!" Victoria wailed. "*I'll* have to come back!"

Martha looked at the floor. "Well, you know what?" she said slowly. "I'll probably have to come back, too. They probably didn't really mean it, about just standing it until Christmas. I don't actually think they really meant it. Don't worry. I'll probably have to come back."

The dark December days passed slowly. Deep snow covered the ground, and icicles glittered in the pale winter sun. Against rules, Victoria and Martha kept their window shut at night; but even so their room was freezing in the morning, and they shivered as they stood together in the doorway for morning inspection.

Almost everyone at Coburn Home School loved the snow and liked to go outdoors after classes. But unless Miss Mossman absolutely made Victoria and Martha go out, they stayed in their room and talked about going home for Christmas. Every afternoon at six o'clock they crossed a day off the calendar.

"In two hours we can cross off another day," Victoria said one afternoon. She picked up the calendar and smiled.

"Oh, vacation will never never never come." Martha groaned. "How many days left?"

"Fifteen. I mean, it will be fifteen days in two hours when I cross off today. That's not so bad, Marth."

But it seemed forever.

One afternoon Victoria received a letter from her aunt who lived in California, and a small package. In the letter her aunt wrote: "I am sending you a small box today. Please be a good, obedient niece and open it right away. It is absolutely to be opened before Christmas. I remembered that when I was a child the weeks before Christmas were long ones. So I am sending you a pre-Christmas present. I am sure you can think of something interesting to do with what is in the box, and perhaps that will make Christmas come more quickly."

"Hey, what a nice aunt!" Martha said.

"She's wonderful," Victoria agreed, opening the package. "Oh, look!"

In the box were twenty little dolls, no bigger than Victoria's thumb. That winter neither Martha nor Victoria especially liked dolls, but these new ones were so small and perfect that both girls loved them at once.

"Martha, I have a good idea," said Victoria.

"What?"

"Help me take the stuff out of this drawer and I'll show you."

They emptied Victoria's lowest drawer and lifted it out of the bureau and put it on the floor. Then Victoria sat down cross-legged beside it.

"What's your idea, Vick?" Martha asked.

"Well, we can divide the drawer with a string or a ruler, or something, and have two corridors, and we can put all the children around and have them in our own boarding school."

It was a delightful game. Martha let the children do all the things she herself wanted to be allowed to do, such as running up and down the corridor, jumping on the beds, and staying up all night.

Victoria pretended that one of the dolls was a beautiful housemother who loved all the children. Victoria had the housemother kiss the children and wave goodbye to them when they went to the school hall in the morning.

"I think this housemother's name is Miss Sweetman,"

Victoria said. "No, it is Miss Sweetland. This house-mother's name is Miss Sweetland."

"Just so long as it isn't Miss Mossman," Martha said. "Once I had a doll named Ruth; but then I knew a girl named Ruth and I didn't like her, so I changed my doll's name to Pearl."

Victoria looked dreamily at the Miss Sweetland doll. "Once I had a dear little doll named Eggy."

"What a terrible name!" Martha said. "Why would you call a doll Eggy? That's awful."

"I don't know," Victoria said vaguely. "But I just loved her. I loved her a lot. Then I had a dog named Moozoo."

Martha looked up from the boarding school. "Named what?"

"Moozoo. He wasn't a real dog. He was a stuffed dog."

"Moozoo," Martha repeated. "You certainly thought up some crazy names all right."

"When I was little, I had the most beautiful rocking horse in the whole world," Victoria said slowly. "He was as big as a real pony, and he had a real mane and a beautiful real tail and stirrups. His name was Ralmadil."

"Hey, that's a good name, for a change," Martha said.

"You know what, Martha?"

"No, what?"

"Ralmadil was the most beautiful rocking horse in the whole world."

"Let's call our boarding school Ralmadil School," Martha suggested.

"All right," Victoria agreed. "Let's."

The Ralmadil School game was a good one, and they played it until Miss Mossman blew the warning whistle for supper.

"Oh, dear," Victoria said regretfully. "That old whistle. We'll have to put the drawer back, but we can leave Ralmadil School right in it if you'll let me put my stuff in one of your bureau drawers. In *our* school we don't have any old whistle blowing ever," she said, and shoved the drawer shut.

"No, we don't," Martha said. "That's a good game, Vick. Let's play it tomorrow."

"All right. Tomorrow we'll take the whole school on a picnic," Victoria decided.

"A picnic? It would be too cold!"

"Oh, it doesn't have to be winter now at our boarding school. It will be nice and warm and sunny, and everybody will go on a big picnic."

"All right," Martha agreed. "Vicky, maybe when we're grown up we could really have our own boarding school and run it ourselves."

"Maybe we could!"

The Ralmadil School game kept them occupied for many afternoons after that, and time passed more quickly. Soon Martha was able to sing:

"Three more days to vacation.
Then we go to the station.

Back to civilization.
Back to Mother and home!"

The day Christmas vacation started, the girls were awakened, not by the usual piercing whistle, but by the distant sound of singing. Then someone ran down the corridor and opened all the doors, and the sound of the music came nearer.

Martha and Victoria sat up in bed in the dark and stared out into the hall.

"Hark! the herald angels sing,
Glory to the new-born King!"

The singing voices came closer and closer, and in the hall shadowy lights began to glow in the winter-morning darkness. Twelve of the older girls, dressed in white and carrying lighted candles, passed down the corridor, singing Christmas carols. It was beautiful to see and hear.

During the bus ride to the station Victoria and Martha said little to each other. Victoria kept playing with the strap of her pocketbook. She put it over her nose, and up over one ear, and finally she put it in her mouth. Martha tried to sit quietly, but she was shivering with excitement. "No more days to vacation!" she whispered to Victoria.

The Double-decker Bed

THE DAY CHRISTMAS VACATION was over Mrs. Coburn called all the girls on Miss Mossman's corridor to a meeting in the drawing room.

"Girls," Mrs. Coburn said, "welcome back to Coburn Home School. I know you will be sorry to hear that Miss Mossman's father is not well and Miss Mossman has decided that she must remain at home with him. Therefore she will not be returning to Coburn School. I know she will miss us all, and certainly we will all miss her. Now I want you to meet your new housemother — someone you will soon learn to know and to love: Miss Caroline Denton."

A tall woman with soft gray hair stood up and smiled. "How do you do, girls?" she said. "I know I will be happy to live here with you, and I hope you will be happy too. I want to learn to know you all, and I hope you girls will always feel free to come to me with any problems you may have. Every day, after the noon meal and before the start of afternoon classes, any of you girls, if you want to, may come to me in my room to talk."

Victoria thought Miss Denton was lovely, and she turned to look at Martha. But Martha was staring at the new housemother, and Martha was frowning.

Miss Denton went on, "I want to say that I think 'Miss Denton' is a rather formal name for your housemother. I'll be happy, I'll be very happy indeed, girls, to have you all call me Mother Carrie, and I hope you will."

Victoria slid down in her chair in embarrassment. Mother Carrie! You couldn't call a perfectly strange woman who was not any relation to you whatsoever any name such as that! Victoria and the other girls left the room slowly.

Martha was waiting for Victoria in the hall. "Ick-en-spick of the most ick," said Martha coldly, and Victoria nodded regretfully.

That night the lights-out signal was given by a bell instead of a whistle. "Hey, a bell! How come, I wonder?" said Martha.

She and Victoria got into their beds and started to whisper.

Victoria was homesick that night, and she wanted to talk about her mother. "Martha," she whispered into the dark, "did I ever tell you about the time my mother let me dress up in her very best dress? She put a big — "

"Yes, you told me," Martha answered. She was sorry

for Victoria, but she didn't want to listen to her when she was homesick. "You did tell me, Vick."

Victoria tried to think of something else to talk about, something in her preboarding-school life. "Martha, I know I never told you about the day my mother took me to a matinee, and afterward we had hot chocolate and — " All of a sudden Victoria stopped talking.

She lay in the dark on her back and began to cry. She tried to stop, but couldn't.

"Vicky," Martha whispered suddenly from the other bed. "Hey, Vick. It's all right if you want to tell me about how your mother let you dress up that time. I don't think you ever told me about *that* time. Go on. Tell me."

Suddenly there was a tap on the door, and a long sliver of light appeared as the door opened slightly. The new housemother must have heard them talking!

"Asleep, girls?" Miss Denton said softly.

There was no answer.

"Good," she said even more softly. She crossed the room with light, quick steps and turned off the radiator. She raised the window and arranged the blind so it wouldn't rattle. She went to Martha's bed and straightened her blankets and tucked them in at the side. Then she went to Victoria's bed and tucked her in, too.

"Sleep well," she whispered, and went out.

Both girls were silent after she left. "Maybe I wouldn't really mind calling her Mother Carrie," thought Victoria. "She's nice." And she fell asleep.

Martha stayed awake a little while longer. She didn't want to admit it even to herself, but she thought the new housemother might not be so bad after all. Then she went to sleep, too.

The next morning, while it was still dark, the housemother came back to their room. She closed the window and turned on the radiator. Then she went to Victoria's bed and put her hand on Victoria's shoulder. "It's morning," she said softly. "Time to get up. Wake up, dear. Breakfast in half an hour!"

Victoria sat up in bed. She was surprised at being wakened so gently. "Why, hello, Miss Denton," she whispered.

The housemother went to Martha's bed and woke her in the same way. "Wake up, Martha. Breakfast in half an hour."

"Hey, no whistle!" said the startled Martha. She heard the steam beginning to hiss into the radiator and saw that the window Miss Denton had opened the night before was now closed. By that time Miss Denton had left their room, and they could hear her going into the next room, closing that window, and turning on that radiator.

"Hey, Vicky!" Martha said, and got out of bed slowly. "What do you think? No inspection!"

"Pretty leebossa," Victoria said.

Within the next few days Miss Denton won the hearts of most of the girls on her corridor. She never used a whistle. When a signal had to be given, she rang a pretty silver bell. Every night she went into each room and told the girls good night. She heard their prayers, too, if they wanted her to listen. Every morning she woke them up after she had turned on the radiators and closed the windows. She really seemed to like children. When they did something wrong, she didn't scold them and wink crossly and give demerits the way Miss Mossman had. Miss Denton seldom was cross at all. Usually the worst thing she said was, "Girls, that's not thoughtful," or, "Girls, you know that is not the right and proper thing to do."

Sue Burton was loud in her praises of Miss Denton and immediately started to call her Mother Carrie. Most of the girls followed Sue's example, for all of them were happier than they had been before. Martha, however, was still on guard; and Victoria, always loyal to Martha, tried not to show her own growing enthusiasm for the new housemother.

One afternoon, just before supper, there was a knock at their door. It was Miss Denton.

"Girls," she said, sitting down, "I've been thinking about this room. It is the smallest room on this corridor, and it is very small for two girls to share."

Martha and Victoria stared at each other in horror. Was it possible that the new housemother was going to separate them?

Miss Denton glanced around the room. "I've suggested to Mrs. Coburn," she went on, "that there will be much more room if we take these out — " and she motioned to the two little white-painted iron beds — "and put in a double-decker bed for you instead. How would you like that?"

How would they like that! A double-decker bed! On rainy afternoons they could hang blankets down from the top bunk and have a playhouse on the bottom one. And at night, after lights-out, they could talk so easily in a double-decker bed! They were ecstatic.

"We'd like it," Martha said. She thought it unwise to let any grownup know what you were really thinking. She knew that the housemother wouldn't want them to talk in bed after lights-out. So she just said again, "Yes, we'd like it very much."

"I know you girls must do a certain amount of whispering in bed after lights-out," Miss Denton said easily. "I don't approve of that, of course, for you need your sleep. But I know you'll probably whisper a little while, and I should think a double-decker bed would be fun. All the rooms will have them eventually, but you may as well have yours now." She smiled pleasantly at them. "Good-bye, girls. I'll see you at supper."

"Jiminy!" Vicky said, after the housemother went out. "Martha, isn't she wonderful?"

Martha looked puzzled. "She *was* nice about people wanting to talk in bed," Martha admitted. "She seems all right. But I'm still not going to call her anything dopey like Mother Carrie."

The Mysterious Nine

By the end of January everyone on the corridor was calling the new housemother Mother Carrie. Everyone, that is, except Martha and Victoria.

Victoria liked the new housemother. But she couldn't quite bring herself to call her Mother Carrie. And Martha still thought the whole thing was ridiculous.

One mild February afternoon after classes, Martha and Victoria stopped to talk with Sue and Edith and Ginny, who were examining an abandoned snow fort made by the older boys. Sue started to argue with Martha about the new housemother. But Martha was stubborn.

"Sue, she's 'sweety-sweety,'" Martha said. "'And I want you all to call me Mother Carrie,'" she mimicked in a sugary voice. Then in her normal tone she added, "And I can't stand the way she says 'Girls, that's not thoughtful.' When she isn't saying that, she's saying, 'Girls, that's not the right and proper thing to do.' That's all she says all the time. It's terrible."

"Martha Sherman, *you're* terrible," Sue said angrily. "She doesn't either say those things all the time. I think Mother Carrie is the sweetest, nicest, loveliest house-mother in the whole wide world."

Victoria sighed. She couldn't agree with Sue completely, but she did feel that Martha was stubborn and unreasonable.

"What's so awful about her saying, 'Girls, that's not thoughtful'?" Victoria asked mildly. "It's better than that Miss Mossman blowing a whistle all the time and winking at you when she got cross. I don't see anything so terrible if she says something isn't thoughtful."

"Oh, Miss Mossman was worse," Martha agreed readily. "But at least she didn't expect us to call her Mother Anything. That would have been really awful. Mother Mossman. Mother Mossman Mossy. Mother Mossman Mossy was so bossy. She blew that whistle all the time and was as sour as a sour old lime."

Martha smiled, pleased with what she had just made up. Then suddenly she stuck her stomach out and marched around alone, singing in a piercing voice:

"Old Mother Mossman Mossy
    Was so bossy.
    She blew that whistle all the time.
    She was as sour as a sour old lime.
    Old Mother Mossman Mossy
    Was so — "

At that moment Miss Denton came along the path. She saw and heard Martha, but Martha didn't see her. Martha continued to stalk around and to sing:

"Old Mother Mossman Mossy
    Was so bossy.
    She blew that whistle all the whole time.
    And she was as sour as a sour old lime.
    Oh, old Mother Mossman Mossy
    Was so bossy — "

"Martha!" Miss Denton was shocked.

Martha whirled around and stood staring at the housemother.

"Martha," Miss Denton said quietly. "That is not kind. That is not a kind thing to shout out, or even to think. Miss Mossman loved you girls very much, and she was sorry to have to leave you."

While the housemother was speaking, Victoria and the other girls stood together silently, not knowing whether to go or stay.

"Well, Martha," Miss Denton continued. "Have you anything to say?"

"I'm sorry," Martha said, her eyes on the ground.

"And I'm sorry, Martha, to have to reprimand you in front of your friends. But you know that what you were singing was not kind. It was not thoughtful." Miss Denton glanced at her watch and smiled briefly at them all, including Martha. "I hope you are truly sorry, dear, and now we will put it out of our minds. I'll see you girls at supper," she added. And she went past them into the dormitory.

At Martha's feet a thin sheet of ice had formed over a small pool of melted snow. Slowly and carefully she picked up the ice and stared through it at the pale winter sky. "Oh, dear!" Martha said. "Why did she have to hear me?" She threw the ice to the ground.

"She was pretty nice about it," Victoria said cautiously. "You have to admit it. She was pretty nice."

"She wasn't so bad," Martha said. "I do admit it. She had to get in that it wasn't thoughtful. But at least she didn't say, 'That's not the right and proper thing to do.'"

At that, Sue and Edith walked off in disgust. Even Victoria thought Martha was terrible. But she stayed with her, and finally Martha began to talk about what she'd like to have for supper. The subject of Miss Denton was dropped.

But Victoria could tell that Martha didn't like Miss Denton any better, no matter how friendly and gentle the housemother's scolding had been.

Victoria often thought that Martha didn't like any of the grownups at Coburn School, with the possible exception of Mr. Hardy, the handy man, and Miss Blanchard, the arithmetic teacher.

Martha liked arithmetic — actually liked it. And she

even seemed to like Miss Blanchard. It was a rule of the
school that roommates could not sit at the same table.
Therefore, at the start of the second term, either Victoria
or Martha had to move from Miss Denton's table. Martha had volunteered to be the one to go, and she had
asked to be put at Miss Blanchard's table.

"How can you like that Miss Blanchard?" Victoria
asked one day. "She's so scary in arithmetic class!"

"I didn't say I liked her," Martha said, gruffly. "But
she isn't so bad."

Victoria couldn't understand it. "She's so red-look-
ing," she persisted. "And her nose is so big. I just don't
know how you can like her so much."

"I never said I liked her so much," Martha said again.
"But she's better than most of the other teachers around
here. And what's so awful about her nose?"

Victoria sighed. "Oh, I just hate arithmetic. I hate it.
I hate everything about it. I even hate the color of the
book."

Lately Victoria had given up even trying to be good
at arithmetic. She had some ideas of her own about
numbers, but they had nothing to do with arithmetic.
For instance, she always thought of certain numbers as
girls and of other numbers as boys. The girls were 1, 3, 5,
7, and 8. The boys were 2, 4, 6, and 9.

The whole idea of some numbers being girls and
other numbers being boys irritated Martha. Martha

couldn't see any sense to it whatever. But it made sense to Victoria. Victoria couldn't possibly have thought of 8 as a boy or of 9 as a girl.

"It's so crazy," Martha argued. "It doesn't make any sense, Vicky. If you had all the odd numbers girls, it might not be so silly. But you have 1, 3, 5, 7, and 8 girls. And if you had the even numbers all boys, 2, 4, 6, and 8. But you have 8 a girl and 9 a boy!"

"Yes, that's right," Victoria said.

"But why? Why don't you have 8 a boy and 9 a girl?"

Victoria shook her head. "I know it sounds silly," she admitted. "But I can't help it. I have the same thing with colors, too."

"What do you mean, with colors?"

"Well, red and yellow are boys, and blue and green are girls."

Martha frowned. "And what's orange?" she asked.

"A boy."

"Lavender?"

"A girl."

"Pink?"

"A boy."

"Gray?"

"Girl."

"Brown?"

"Boy."

Martha thought for a moment. "All right," she said finally. "But I should think green would be a boy."

"Well, it's not," Victoria said sharply. "It's a girl."

"Vick, couldn't you change on the numbers and have 8 a boy?" Martha said suddenly. She never gave up easily.

But Victoria couldn't change that. And she went on hating arithmetic.

One day after classes Martha said, "I just found out a good thing in arithmetic. Want to hear it?"

"What do you mean: a good thing?" Victoria was doubtful.

"A good thing. Take any two numbers." Martha tried to ignore Victoria's woebegone expression. "Go on. Take any two numbers under 10."

"All right," Victoria sighed. "1 and 3." She took a couple of girls.

"Now reverse them."

"What?"

"Just reverse them. Look, you took 1 and 3 — 13. Reverse them and you have 3 and 1 — 31."

"All right." Victoria nodded.

"Now take the smaller from the larger."

"Oh, Martha!"

"Go on, Vicky. This is good. It really is. Take 13 from 31."

Victoria looked depressed. She couldn't do that subtraction in her head.

"How much is 13 from 31? It's 18," Martha said.

"All right."

"And 18 is evenly divisible by 9. That means 9 goes into 18 twice even — exactly twice." Martha looked pleased.

"Well, what's so wonderful about that?" Victoria was puzzled.

"What's so good about it is that you can take any two numbers under 10, reverse them, take the smaller from the larger, and the result is always evenly divisible by 9. Isn't that good? It doesn't matter what any old numbers you take. It always works out that way: always goes into the result evenly. Isn't that good?"

Victoria was still bewildered. Martha tried it again, with 7 and 2, and with 4 and 8, and with 6 and 9. No matter what two numbers Martha took, when she reversed them and took the smaller from the larger, 9 always went into the result evenly. Finally Victoria admitted that it was rather interesting. "It's sort of mysterious, Marth," she said. "Does it work with any other number?"

"No, just with 9. Isn't it a good thing?"

"Yes, sort of," Victoria agreed. "I wonder why it works. And I wonder why it works with 9, and not with 7, for instance."

"I don't know for sure," Martha said. "But I'll ask her sometime."

"Ask who?"

"Miss Blanchard. She told me about it."

"Miss Blanchard told you a good thing like that?" Victoria was amazed.

"Sure she did. She's an all-right teacher, Vicky. She knows a lot of good things. You're silly to be scared of her."

"It certainly is funny, you sticking up for a teacher," Victoria said slowly.

"I'm not sticking up for her. I wouldn't stick up for any of the old teachers here!"

"Well, you're sticking up for Miss Blanchard."

"I am not. Anyhow, you're always sticking up for that Miss Denton."

"Oh, Miss Denton's nice, Martha. She really is. Don't you like her at all?"

But all Martha would say was, "Ick-en-spick."

Old Tooth

Victoria's birthday was February 6. At home her mother had made that date seem of great importance. However, at Coburn School February 6 proved to be just like every other day. Victoria's birthday package, containing books, a blue sweater, blue mittens, and a new pencil box, had arrived two days early, and she had opened it at once. So on her birthday she had no presents to open. At supper the other children all sang "Happy birthday, dear Victoria," and there was a birthday cake for her table. But the day wasn't at all like her birthdays at home.

However, it was good to be nine years old. Martha's birthday was in August, and therefore she had been nine for six months.

Martha and Victoria did not often think about the difference in their ages. Victoria had had a governess the summer before she went to Coburn School, and, except in arithmetic, she was not behind Martha in schoolwork. But once in awhile, especially when she was homesick and cried, Martha thought that Victoria did act young.

Sometimes it seemed to Martha that Victoria acted even younger than she was. For instance, after supper one night, when Martha and Victoria and Edith were standing in the hall talking to Miss Denton, Victoria announced that she'd lost a back tooth that afternoon.

"I'm going to put it under my pillow tonight," she said happily.

"You're going to put it under your *pillow!*" Edith Scott said. "Why would you do such a crazy thing with an old tooth?"

Victoria looked at Edith in surprise. "Why, I always put a tooth under my pillow and get a present. Don't you?"

"Oh, my goodness!" Edith Scott groaned. "I did that when I was little, but you don't believe that stuff any more, do you?"

"What sort of present, dear?" Miss Denton asked. She smiled at Victoria.

Martha, embarrassed, stared at the floor. Suddenly Victoria became embarrassed, too. She looked up at Miss Denton and tried to smile as though she hadn't really meant what she had said. The subject was dropped, to Martha's great relief.

That night in bed, after Miss Denton had told them good night, Martha began to whisper. "Hey, Vicky, what did you do with that old tooth?"

Victoria didn't answer.

"All right. Don't tell me." Martha was a little angry.

"Well, I'm sorry, Martha," Victoria said. "I'm very sorry, but it just so happens that I think you're very mean. And so is Edith Scott."

"What presents did you ever get?"

It was easier to discuss it in the dark, in the privacy of the top bunk of the double-decker bed. So Victoria told her. "Well, once I got a tiny little doll. And once I got a little book. And I got a little ring with an amethyst. And once they left a pretty little locket. And the last time they — "

"Oh!" Martha couldn't stand it any longer. "Who's *they?* Your mother just put that stuff under your pillow. Do you believe in *fairies* or something? Ick-en-spick!"

"Martha Sherman, don't you say 'ick-en-spick' to me!" Victoria was angry now. As for the fairies, for a long time now she'd known that there probably weren't any fairies. But sometimes she wasn't exactly sure. At any rate, she didn't want to discuss it any more with Martha.

"Good night," she said, and turned over on her stomach.

"Good night."

There was silence for a few moments.

"Vicky, you asleep?"

"Yes, I am."

"I'm sorry I said 'ick-en-spick' to you," Martha whispered.

"It's all right," Victoria said. "It's all right, Martha." And then they went to sleep.

The next morning, after the housemother woke them, Martha went to get washed first. When she came back from the bathroom, Victoria was sitting up in bed, looking at something in her hand.

"What's the matter?" Martha asked as she hung up her towel and washcloth.

"It's just so funny!" Victoria said. She sounded puzzled.

"What's so funny?"

"It's a quarter! I never got money before. I always got a little present."

Martha couldn't believe it. "Is your tooth gone?" she asked finally.

"Of course my tooth is gone," Victoria said. "But I'm so surprised to have them leave me a quarter!"

Martha looked at it. Then she grinned. "Well, look at that!" she said. "Miss Denton must have put it there, Vicky. She must have!"

Victoria looked up at Martha. "Yes, I guess she did," she said slowly. She looked back at the quarter, and suddenly she realized that of course her mother had always just pretended that fairies left the presents. "I guess she must have. That was pretty leebossa of her, you know it?"

Martha tried to sound casual. "Oh, it was all right," she said.

They heard Miss Denton's voice in the corridor, and
Victoria jumped out of bed and ran to the door. "Could
I speak to you a minute?" she said to the housemother.

Miss Denton came in and smiled at her. "Yes, dear?
Better start dressing. You're late!"

Victoria looked at the floor. "I guess you put the quarter under my pillow," she said. "Thank you."

The housemother looked at her for a moment. "Why,
Victoria," she said finally, "don't you — "

"I know you put it there," Victoria said shyly. She
looked up and smiled. "Thank you. Thanks a lot."

Miss Denton put her hand on Victoria's head. "Well,
dear — "

Martha interrupted. "I guess she doesn't believe that
baby stuff any more," she said.

"Don't you, Victoria?" Miss Denton asked.

"No, not any more," Victoria answered.

The housemother smiled again and turned to go. At
the door she looked back at Vicky. "You know, dear,
you're growing up a little bit every day. Gradually
you'll stop believing in some things. But as you grow up
you will find there are many lovelier things to believe
in, Victoria."

The girls glanced at each other, slightly puzzled.

The housemother continued, "As you grow up, there
will be more wonderful things to believe in — things
which are true as well as wonderful." She looked

thoughtful. "Well, girls, get dressed now," she added briskly, and went out.

Victoria picked up her towel and washcloth and went to the bathroom. Martha started to dress slowly, lost in thought. That old Miss Denton wasn't so bad, she had to admit. She really had to admit it.

The Feast

For some time Martha had been thinking that they ought to have a midnight feast. "It's always supposed to be so much fun to go to boarding school and have midnight feasts," she said gloomily. "And we never have any at this old boarding school. I guess we have to have one. Who'll we ask, Vick?"

"We could ask True and Edith and Ginny," Victoria suggested. "And Sue and Eleanor?"

"All right, we'll ask them."

"What will we have to eat, Marth?"

"Oh, I don't know. What do people have at midnight feasts? I guess ice cream, and some of those good pickles, and cake, and cookies, and some orange drink. What do you think?"

"Maybe we could have some sardines," Victoria said. "But I guess Miss Denton wouldn't let us eat sardines."

"Oh, Vicky!" Martha exploded. "What's Miss Denton going to have to do with our midnight feast? You're crazy! She isn't even going to know about it!"

"Oh, yes, you're right," Victoria said. The idea of the midnight feast did not appeal to her, and she hoped that Martha would forget about it. But Martha didn't. She began to make her plans at once and to issue invitations.

"We're going to have a midnight feast in our room next Wednesday," she said to Edith Scott after breakfast the next day. "You want to come?"

Edith's round red-brown eyes opened wide. "Oh, Martha, you're terrible. How could we have a midnight feast?"

"Vicky and I are having it," Martha corrected her politely. "If you don't want to come, just say so. We're going to ask True and Ginny and El and Sue, too."

"Well, I don't know. What are you going to have to eat?" Edith asked.

"Cake and ice cream and pickles and orange drink and, oh, some other stuff. Candy. Cookies. Maybe sardines."

Edith thought it over. "Well, all right. I'll come," she said. "When is it?"

"Wednesday. We told you."

"But what time Wednesday?"

"Midnight, you crazy! When else would you have a midnight feast?"

"Well." There was a long pause. "Well, all right. I'll come."

"Some dumb girl," Martha said as she and Vicky walked away to the school hall.

By the end of the day Martha had asked the other guests. Everyone except Ginny Frost accepted. Ginny said that her mother didn't allow her to eat between meals. She always brought her mother into every conversation. Sue, Eleanor, and True did not want to come, but they didn't want to make Martha angry. So they accepted her invitation.

Victoria never knew how Martha smuggled in the food for the midnight feast. She thought Mr. Hardy must have helped. Ever since the Halloween Party he had been friendly with Martha. At any rate, however she did it, Wednesday afternoon Martha brought the food into their room and hid it in the closet.

After supper, just before the singing, Martha whispered reminders to the guests. "Come to our room at midnight," she said. "Don't forget."

Usually Victoria wanted to whisper in bed even longer than Martha wanted to, and when Martha went to sleep first, Victoria often lay awake making up interesting adventures. But that night she was so sleepy she did not see how she could possibly stay awake until midnight. She tried to carry on a whispered conversation with Martha, but in the middle of it she fell asleep. Martha got out of bed and shook Victoria's shoulder.

"Oh, please, Vicky!" Martha whispered. "You just can't go to sleep now! Wake up! It's only nine-thirty!"

"I'm sorry," Victoria said sleepily. "Let's talk about

something exciting." But in a minute she fell asleep again, and once more Martha had to shake her awake.

"Listen, Vick," Martha whispered. "I'll tell you a real scary story about — "

"Oh, no, don't! I'm awake," Victoria assured her quickly. "I'm awake. Let's talk about something interesting." She sat up in bed and tried to think of something interesting. But she began to yawn, in spite of herself, and she lay down again.

Martha climbed up to the upper bunk and sat beside Victoria. "Now, stay awake!" she said. "I'll tell you some more about Richy."

"All right," Victoria whispered happily. She loved to hear about Richy, although she did not know him. Richy lived in New York in the apartment house where Martha's family lived. He was thirteen years old, and he could draw wonderful pictures, and he could carve things out of wood, and in the summer he chewed tar he dug out of the street.

"Well," Martha began. "Once Richy went to the circus alone and he saw the side show. He saw the Fat Woman, and he saw Coo-Coo the Bird Girl, and he saw a man who swallowed swords. My mother never would let me see the side show, but Richy saw it. And then once my uncle took Richy and me to Coney Island and we rode on the roller coaster."

"My mother and I rode on a Ferris wheel once," Victoria said sleepily.

"Oh, a roller coaster is much better. I wonder what time it is."

Martha slid down from the top bunk and looked at the clock. Only ten! Two more hours until time for the midnight feast! Martha was tired, too. Victoria was again sound asleep.

Martha sat on the edge of her bed in the dark and wondered what to do. She was discouraged and lonely. Finally she decided to have the feast at eleven o'clock, instead of at midnight, and she tiptoed down the hall to notify the guests of the new time. Sleepily they promised to stay awake and come to the feast at eleven.

Martha was so sleepy herself that she lay down on top of the covers on her bed. Every few minutes she kicked the springs of the top bunk, to keep Victoria awake. Every time Martha kicked, Victoria woke up and said, "All right, I'm awake."

Just before eleven o'clock Martha lit her flashlight and took the food out of the closet. The container of ice cream was soft, and ice cream dripped slowly from it. Martha spread her raincoat on the floor and placed the ice cream in the middle of it. She took the cake out of the box and put it beside the ice cream. Around them on the raincoat she arranged the pickles, the fruit juice, the cookies and candy, and the sardines. Then she turned off her flashlight and lay down again to wait for the guests.

There was a loud crash, and she sat bolt upright in

bed. It was morning! Miss Denton stood in the middle of the room. When the housemother had come in, her foot had struck the glass jar of fruit juice. The jar had spun across the room and crashed into the radiator, and now the fruit juice spread in a slow stream across the floor. In the dim light Martha and Miss Denton looked around the room. The ice cream had melted out of the flimsy container. It had flowed over the raincoat and onto the rug. Silently the housemother looked at the melted ice cream and the slowly spreading fruit juice, the sardines, the cake, the candy, the pickles.

"Well, Martha," she said at last. "What is the meaning of this?"

Martha looked away.

"Martha, what is the meaning of this?" the housemother repeated.

"I just wanted to have a midnight feast," Martha said slowly.

"A midnight feast! You should not have done this, Martha." The housemother's voice was stern.

Martha nodded miserably.

"Did anyone else come to this midnight feast, or was it just for you and Victoria?"

"We did ask some other kids," Martha said. "But they didn't come. They went to sleep. And Vicky went to sleep. And I guess I went to sleep, too. Anyhow, no one came, and we didn't have it." She sighed. "Vicky didn't want to have it, anyhow. No one else did. Don't get mad at them."

"Martha, what in the world made you decide to have a midnight feast?"

Martha tried to shrug in her old carefree way. "Oh, at boarding school you're supposed to have all these wonderful midnight feasts," she muttered. "So I thought we ought to have one."

"Oh, Martha, Martha. You thought you were 'supposed' to have a midnight feast!" The housemother sighed. "You go out of your way not to do so many things you really are supposed to do." She spoke as though to herself, or to another grownup. Her voice was sad.

Victoria woke up and leaned over the edge of her bed. "I'm sorry," she whispered to them both.

"You girls should not have done this, Victoria," the housemother said. "I am disappointed in you both. I'll talk to you later, but now you must pick up this food and clean up the floor. I'll get a mop and some cloths." She shook her head and went out.

That afternoon, after classes, Miss Denton called them both to her room. "I've decided that the failure of your plans is punishment enough for you this time," she said. "But I hope you will learn a lesson from this experience. I don't know that you will. However, I am not going to punish you."

"Thank you," Martha said sincerely.

"I do want to talk to you girls briefly about something

I think of often. I am fond of you two, as I am fond of every child on my corridor. I enjoy you girls, and I think it is fine that in many ways you make up your own minds and do not copy others. The world will always need those who do not try to be just like everyone else." She stopped and looked at them. Then she went on. "But there is a happy medium between the child who wants to be just like everyone else and the child who refuses to do anything the way other children do. I hope, with all my heart, that you girls will be able to find that happy medium in the months and years ahead." She stopped again and sighed. She knew they were not hearing what she was trying to say to them. "You may go now," she said quietly.

Outside her room, Martha gave a sigh of relief.

"Glad that's over," she remarked. "Pretty ick-en-spick lecture, if you ask me."

"I think she's pretty leebossa, if you ask *me*," Victoria said rather coldly. The midnight feast was not mentioned again between them.

Mother Carrie

In March the snow and ice melted, and the bare black branches of the trees, shining with moisture, glittered against a blue and cloudless sky. The children still had to wear their heavy coats, for the air was cold. But they stuffed their mittens in their pockets, and their hands felt cool and free in the March sunshine. Little streams of icy water rushed across the spongy ground, and only on the brown hills were there still patches of snow.

"The hills look sort of like a bowl of cornflakes," Victoria said dreamily to Martha, "after you've put a lot of sugar on but before you've put the milk on."

One windy March day, down at the swings, Victoria started to talk about Miss Denton. Martha was swinging and Victoria was pushing her.

"I think Miss Denton's nice, Martha," Victoria said. She gave an especially strong push.

Martha was silent.

"Marth, wouldn't you *ever* want to call her Mother Carrie?"

80

Martha was still silent, but Victoria could tell she was thinking about it. "I don't think so," Martha said finally. "It just sounds so dumb."

"Everyone else calls her that, Marth," Victoria said. "It's silly for us to be the only people to say Miss Denton."

"Well, just because Ginny Frost and Sue Burton and that dopey Edith Scott call her Mother Carrie is no reason for *us* to call her that!"

Victoria sighed. She certainly wished Martha didn't always think it was terrible to do anything the way anyone else did it. Victoria had made up her mind that she was going to call the housemother Mother Carrie. She didn't look forward to telling Martha, but she knew she had to give her some warning.

"Well, Martha, I have to tell you," she said slowly, still pushing the swing. "I'm going to call her Mother Carrie."

Silently Martha pumped while Victoria pushed.

"I really like her," Victoria said. "She's nice. She really is."

"If you love your own mother so much, how can you call someone else Mother *Anybody?*" Martha asked in a strained voice.

"I thought about that," Victoria said. She was glad to have a chance to discuss it. "I thought about that. I couldn't call her just plain 'Mother,' of course. But 'Mother Carrie' is all right. We're not with our own mothers now, and Mother Carrie is our housemother at this school, and she *is* very mothery to us. You *have* to admit that. Miss Mossman never came in and told us good night. She just blew that whistle. Miss Mossman never woke us up in the morning. She never closed our window and turned on the radiator. And it was always so cold. . . ." She stopped and thought bleakly of those dark, freezing mornings. "But Mother Carrie closes our window and turns on the radiator and — "

"Hey, you're calling her Mother Carrie already, Vicky. Did you hear yourself?" Martha asked wonderingly.

"Well, I'm sorry, Martha, I really am," Victoria said. "But I just can't help it. It just seems all right and sort of natural and — "

"You mean it seems the right and proper thing to do?" Martha sounded suddenly sarcastic. But then her tone changed. "Oh, all right, Vicky. Go ahead and call her that. You want to, so go ahead."

"You're not mad?"

"No, I'm not. Honest." Martha brought the swing to a slow stop and stood up. Then she lay across the swing on her stomach and turned herself around and around, with her feet on the ground, until the chain was completely twisted. "No, I'm not," she repeated. She lifted her feet off the ground, and the chain, untwisting rapidly, spun her around in circles. When it stopped she stood up, staggering a little. "No, honestly, I don't care," she said. "I still think it's a dopey name, but go ahead. Now I'll push you for a while. Get on."

Victoria was relieved and happy as she swung back and forth in the cold March air. She'd made up her own mind. And she'd told Martha. And Martha wasn't mad.

When Miss Denton came to their room to say good night, she went first, as usual, to turn off the radiator and open the window. Then she leaned over Martha in the lower bunk. "Good night, Martha," she whispered, and tucked in the blanket. "Sleep tight."

"Good night," Martha said. "I will." And she pulled her head down low on her pillow.

Miss Denton straightened up and looked at Victoria in the upper bunk. Victoria raised herself on one elbow.

"Good night, Vicky," the housemother said softly.

"Good night." Victoria leaned forward. "Good night, Mother Carrie," she whispered. "I'm going to call you that now."

"Good night, dear," the housemother said. "Sleep well." And that was all. It hadn't been a bit ick-en-spick, thought Victoria as she went to sleep.

The Hut

In April, Martha and Victoria began to wake up early every morning. They wanted to get up at five-thirty and go outdoors. But no one was allowed to get out of bed before six-thirty, and since the disastrous midnight feast Martha and Victoria were making a real effort not to break any rules.

One morning, when they were whispering to each other at five-thirty, Martha said, "We could at least get dressed now and be all ready to go outdoors when it's six-thirty. We could get dressed in *bed*."

"But how can we get our clothes without getting out of bed?"

"I can reach my underwear drawer from here. I can't reach yours, but you can wear some of mine." Martha leaned out of bed, pulled open one of her bureau drawers, threw underwear and socks up to Victoria, and took out some for herself. Both girls dressed silently.

"Finished?" Martha whispered.

"Yes, but how can we get our outside things?"

Martha looked at the clothes they had put on their

chairs the night before. They were supposed to hang them in the closet, but if they put them, neatly folded, on the backs of their chairs, the housemother didn't object.

"Hey, look!" Martha whispered suddenly. She reached under her bed and pulled out a long, thin stick of wood. She had been saving it for weeks. She had known it would come in handy sometime. After a few unsuccessful attempts, she hooked it under Victoria's skirt and tossed the skirt up to Victoria. Next she fished for and caught Victoria's blouse. Then she slowly lifted her own skirt and blouse from her chair and pulled them onto her bed.

At six-thirty both girls jumped out of bed, fully dressed except for their shoes. They ran to the bathroom to wash, dashed back to their room, combed their hair, and hurried downstairs. They were outdoors at twenty minutes to seven.

They started to walk toward the little wood in back of Shippen Hall.

"We can look for some violets," Victoria suggested.

"No violets yet," Martha said. "But we can look, of course. You know what, Vicky?" she said thoughtfully as they walked into the wood. "We could ask permission to get up early every morning for awhile, and we could come out here before breakfast every morning, if she'll let us. And — " here Martha spoke very slowly — "we could build a hut."

"Build a hut!" Victoria repeated huskily. "Marth, do you think she'd let us?"

"We'll ask her tonight after lights-out," Martha said. "Let's look around for a good place to build it."

Sunlight fell on them through the pale green leaves of maple and birch as they wandered through the little wood.

"How about here?" Martha pointed to a small open space among the trees. "We could use that tree stump as a table, and that fallen-over tree as part of the back wall."

Victoria, standing in the early-morning sunshine in the little clearing, was silent and happy. She had never helped to build a hut before, but she couldn't wait to begin.

When it was time for breakfast they left the wood and walked to the dining room. They didn't talk about the hut. But off and on all during that sunny spring day they thought about the hut they were going to build, and they made their plans.

When Miss Denton came to their room to say good night, Martha told her that they'd dressed in bed that morning so that they could go outdoors as early as possible.

"May we please have permission to get up early and go out in the mornings?" Martha asked.

The housemother thought it over. "It is beautiful early in the morning now," she said at last. "You girls need your rest, but if you wake up early anyway — "

Martha took a deep breath. "We want to build a hut," she explained. "Don't tell anyone, but that's what we want to do. Please let us!"

"Build a hut? Where?"

"In the woods in back of here. Please let us. Please say yes!"

The housemother looked at them and then out the window. Finally she said, "Well, all right. If you are both so quiet you won't wake anyone, you may dress early and go out at six o'clock. But not one minute earlier! And you must absolutely tiptoe down the stairs, and open and close the front door quietly. Will you promise?"

"We promise. Thank you very much."

"Good night, girls."

"Good night."

Martha began to whisper first. "Hey, Vick. Maybe we can finish the hut before spring vacation!"

"Seventeen days."

"We can finish it long before. Then I can tell Richy about it!"

"This time tomorrow it will be only sixteen days," Victoria said. She was longing for it to be time to go home to see her mother.

"That's plenty of time. I can't wait to tell Richy. You know what, Vicky?"

"No, what?"

"Richy had that secret language first. He made up ick-en-spick and leebossa."

"He did?" Victoria was amazed.

"Yes, he did. I just made up ankendosh."

Victoria leaned over the edge of her bed and tried to look at Martha in the dark. "But I thought you despised to copy anybody!"

"Well, I do. But Richy's different."

"Oh." Victoria pulled herself back into her bed. "Anyhow, ankendosh is good, too," she said. "I wish I could make up a word sometime."

"Maybe you can. Anyhow, tomorrow we'll start our hut."

The next morning at six o'clock they tiptoed down the stairs and walked quietly down the graveled path to the woods.

"What'll we do first?" Martha said. She studied the place they had selected. "We'll have to figure out what to use for walls."

She looked at the fallen tree. It still had a few branches on it. "Let's look around for some old boards, Vicky. We can nail them on those branches."

"I don't think Mother Carrie will let us do much nailing," Victoria said.

"Probably not," Martha agreed. "But we can lean some flat boards against those branches somehow, and maybe tie them. We don't care if the rain comes in."

"When we get some walls, maybe we could use my old raincoat for the roof," Victoria suggested.

"Leebossa," said Martha.

Five days later they had quite a lot done on the hut. The branches of the fallen tree served as sturdy props to hold the flat boards. Mr. Hardy had let them have two large, thin, wooden, bicycle crates, and those made excellent side walls.

They brought out Victoria's old raincoat and Martha climbed up on the tree-stump table, which was now in the center of the hut, and draped the raincoat over the tops of the tree walls. Then she and Victoria stood in front of the hut and looked it over.

"Now we just need a front wall and some sort of a door," Martha said.

For several days work on the hut was at a standstill. They couldn't think of what to use for a front wall and a door. Finally Victoria suggested that they ask for permission to walk down the road to the old Perry place. No one had lived there for years, and though the students at Coburn School were not permitted to go into the house or even up on the sagging porch, they were sometimes allowed to wander around the fields beside the Perry house.

"Maybe we'll get an idea there, anyhow," Victoria said hopefully.

They received permission for their walk, and after

classes they hurried away. At least Victoria hurried, and tried to urge Martha to walk faster too. But Martha was in an unusually silent, listless mood. She didn't want to admit it, but she was discouraged.

At the Perry place she became gloomier. "Look at that old haunted house," she said.

"Oh, do you think it's haunted?" Victoria asked.

"Of course not. But it looks awful, doesn't it?"

They stared up at the house, at the torn blinds, the broken front steps, the unpainted gray shingles, the crumbling chimney.

"I haven't had any good ideas yet," Martha said in a hollow voice.

"Come on!" Victoria didn't want to stand there any longer. "Come on! Let's go around in back. We'll have a good idea. I almost know it."

But Martha continued to stare mournfully at the house. "Maybe the Perrys are still living inside there," she said. "Maybe they're still inside. And all they have to eat is cold rice pudding because their chimney is broken and they can't even have a fire in their old dusty fireplace." She stopped for a moment, lost in thought. "Their fireplace is full of old cobwebs," she added, warming to her story. "It's full of old cobwebs, and the chimney is broken, and they just sit there and eat cold old rice pudding. And the floor creaks and — "

"Oh, Martha!" Victoria couldn't bear to hear any more. "Come on. Let's look around in back."

They went behind the house and walked along a little path overgrown with weeds. Suddenly Victoria found what she'd wanted them to find, without having known exactly what it would be. It was the old Perry dump heap.

"Oh, leebossa," Martha muttered as she realized what it was. "Oh, lee-lee-lee-lee-lee-leebossa," she chanted softly.

They poked at the dump heap and kicked aside some old galoshes and old pieces of wire. They pulled out a torn piece of carpet and tossed aside a dirty Indian blanket. They walked around the dump heap and prodded and pushed. They found old magazines and old shoes and rusted tin cans. And at last they uncovered a weather-beaten door. It had no doorknob, and one of the boards was missing. But it was a door.

Victoria took one end, Martha took the other, and they walked around the Perry house and set off down the road back to school. Martha looked back at the Perry house and ducked her head politely. "Thank you," she said. "Enjoy your cold rice pudding."

The next morning everything went more easily. Mr. Hardy offered them a small wooden crate which was wide enough for the front wall when they put the door beside it.

"Now we need a window," Victoria said. "So we can sit in here and read, and so we can look out when we want to."

A window was a difficult problem. Several times Mr. Hardy had offered to help them. But Martha thought they should figure out the window themselves. One morning she asked Mr. Hardy to lend her his saw, and he refused. He said that he'd be glad to lend the saw to her if the school belonged to him. But, he said flatly, he couldn't lend the saw to her in view of the fact that the school did not belong to him. "Why do you want it?" he asked casually.

"I just want to make a window," Martha told him. "If you'll just lend me your old saw, I can saw one of the boards in the back wall and make a window space there. Vicky can hold the board so the wall won't come down."

"Tell you what," Mr. Hardy said. "You won't let me saw it for you, and I can't let you take my saw and saw it yourself. But I can hold the board for you and just put my other hand on top of yours while you do the sawing. That way, you do the sawing, but I don't let you take my saw. How's that? That a fair proposition?"

"I think it is a fair proposition, Mr. Hardy," Victoria said. "Don't you, Marth?"

"Oh, all right. It's a fair proposition," Martha agreed.

"I'll meet you there with the saw at three-thirty," Mr. Hardy promised.

After school they went to the hut. Martha stood on a crate Mr. Hardy had brought, and he held the board she was going to saw. The sawing took a long time, but finally Martha did saw through the board on a slant, and a triangular piece of wood dropped out of the back wall. She handed the saw back to Mr. Hardy, thanked him, then ran around to the front of the hut. She and Victoria went in, pulled the front door shut, and sat down on the ground beside the tree-stump table.

"Light enough?" Mr. Hardy called in to them.

"It's just lovely!" Victoria said, looking around happily.

They sat on a carpet of pine needles beside their table, and sunlight came through the three-cornered window and shone on them both.

"Take a look, Mr. Hardy," Martha called. "Look at us in our hut!"

Mr. Hardy's face appeared at the window and he grinned at them. Then he withdrew his head. "Well, so long," he called.

"Good-bye, and thanks a lot, Mr. Hardy!" they shouted.

"Oh, I wish we could just live here," Martha said, and lay down in the sunlight on the pine needles.

"So do I," Vicky said. "Isn't it a beautiful hut, Martha?"

Martha looked around. "It is," she agreed. "We have to figure out some furniture now, but anyhow the hut is finished. And it's beautiful."

The Visit

"Six more days till vacation!" Victoria sang as she ran upstairs one afternoon after classes. She put her books and Martha's in their room and turned to go out again. Mother Carrie stood in the doorway, with a piece of paper in her hand. She came in and sat down, and drew Victoria to her.

"Vicky," she said, "your mother has just written me that she has to go out of town again next week. She is very disappointed and unhappy. She wanted me to tell you, dear. She is writing you, too."

Victoria stared at the housemother in disbelief. "But she'll be back in time for spring vacation," she finally said, firmly.

"No, dear, she won't be back in time. That's why she is so disappointed. I'm sorry, Vicky."

Victoria continued to stare at the housemother. "But what'll I do?" Victoria said. Her voice rose. "What'll I *do?*" she cried. And then she burst into tears.

Mother Carrie put her arms around her. "I know how you feel, dear," she said. "But we can have a good time here, Vicky. Some of the other girls are going to spend their vacation here, you know, and we can all have a happy time together."

"But I want to see my mother!" Victoria wailed. She knew she was acting like a baby, but she couldn't help it. "I want to see my mother!" she cried again.

"And you will, darling," Mother Carrie said. "Your mother wants me to tell you that as soon as she comes back from her trip she is going to come up here to see you for a whole day. Now, won't that be grand? Now, isn't that something lovely to look forward to? Your mother is going to come to see you the very first Saturday after she comes back. And you'll have the whole day with her."

Victoria tried to stop crying. "Will she really come?" she said.

"Yes, Victoria. She will really come. Are you going outdoors now, dear?" the housemother asked, standing up.

"I have to meet Martha at our hut," Victoria said listlessly.

"Well, wear your blue sweater, will you? It's a little cool today," Mother Carrie said. "And even if it were not cool I'd want you to wear that pretty blue sweater. Do you know why?"

"No, why?"

"Because it makes your eyes so blue," the house-mother said.

"It does?" Victoria asked with interest.

"Yes, it certainly does. Now put it on and go meet Martha."

They went downstairs together, slowly. "You know, Vicky," Mother Carrie said at the front door, "it is self-ish of me, but I'm glad you'll be here with me. I know how much your mother will miss you. But I will love to have you here with me."

"You will?" Victoria said.

In spite of her disappointment about spring vaca-tion, she was so pleased with what Mother Carrie had said that she repeated the entire conversation to Martha. She repeated it several times.

That spring vacation was not so unpleasant after all. The few girls who had not been able to go home all sat at one big table in the dining room. There were no classes, of course, and the children played outdoors all day long. In the evenings Mother Carrie read aloud to them after supper. So the vacation passed quite happily for Victoria, and soon it was over. Martha came back, and life returned to normal.

One morning a letter came from Mrs. North, saying that she would arrive the following Saturday.

"Martha!" Victoria cried, waving the letter. "My

mother's coming this Saturday and she'll stay until late in the afternoon, and she says she wants to meet Mother Carrie and everyone and especially you!"

"Me! What'd she say?"

"She says — wait a minute until I find the place — here it is. She says, 'I'm especially eager to meet your little friend Martha.'"

"'Little friend,'" Martha repeated, and made a face.

Victoria reread her mother's letter, and then she put it away in the drawer in which she kept every letter her mother had written her. It was wo⸳⸳ ⸳rul to have her mother's visit to look forward to. But she wondered how her mother would like Martha. Victoria loved Martha. She hoped her mother would like her, too. But she wasn't at all sure that she would.

On Saturday, when Mrs. North stepped out of the taxi, Victoria who had been waiting on the porch steps for an hour, hurled herself toward her mother, tripped on the steps, and fell on the gravel driveway.

Mrs. North picked her up. "Darling, did you hurt yourself?" she cried, and tried to examine her daughter's knees. But Victoria pulled her inside the house and introduced her to Mother Carrie and to Mrs. Coburn, and also to two of the older girls who were reading downstairs. Then Victoria took her mother upstairs to show her their room. Martha had disappeared.

Mrs. North looked at Victoria's knees and saw they were all right. Then she sat down and looked around.

"It's a sweet little room, dear," she said. "But Mother is worried about the double-decker bed. Why don't you sleep in the lower one? I'm so afraid you may fall out of the top one, dear. Martha is older than you are, and I think that perhaps she should have the upper bunk."

"Oh, Mother, no! She *lets* me have the top one. The bottom one isn't nearly so much fun. Please don't talk about it in front of her!"

"Well, all right," Mrs. North said reluctantly. "Now sit down beside me, darling, and let me look at you."

They talked for awhile. Victoria showed her mother her arithmetic book, which, her mother agreed, looked very hard. Next Victoria showed the marbles Sue had given her in exchange for Victoria's blue fountain pen. Her mother said she thought Victoria should have kept the fountain pen, but she didn't scold her. Then Victoria took her mother over to the school hall and showed her the library.

At dinner they sat at Mrs. Coburn's table. Mrs. North was tall and slim, and she wore a lovely blue dress and a broad-brimmed black straw hat. Victoria was sure she was the prettiest mother who had ever visited the school.

After dinner Mrs. North suggested that she and Victoria and Martha go for a walk together.

Victoria went to find Martha, and although Martha didn't want to go for a walk, she said she would come. They started down the road toward the old Perry house. Mrs. North walked between the girls, swinging Victoria's hand. She held out a hand to Martha, too, but Martha trudged along with both hands awkwardly stuck in her belt. No one said anything for a long time.

Finally Mrs. North turned to Martha and said pleasantly, "Do your parents live in New York, dear?"

"Yes, they do," Martha said. "On West Sixty-fourth Street." She gave a big sigh and added, "Oh, boy-o-boy, I'll sure be glad to get home again. Boy, I'll sure be glad to get home from this place!"

Victoria was puzzled by the way Martha was talking. She had never before said "Oh, boy-o-boy." And she spoke in an unfamiliar, hoarse voice. Victoria looked up at her mother. She did want her to like Martha!

"What an odd old house!" Mrs. North said, looking at the old Perry place ahead of them on the right. "I love old deserted houses. Do you think we could look in a window?"

"Sure, why not?" said Martha. "Sure!"

Mrs. North took off her hat and put it on the ground. She ran her hands over her lovely fair hair and then stepped to one of the windows and peered in. "I love old houses," she said again.

Martha and Victoria stood watching her for a few moments. Then Martha began to hunt around for a good strong blade of grass to put between her thumbs and blow on. She had recently learned to make a loud noise that way, and she liked to make it.

As Mrs. North turned away from the window, Sue Burton and Eleanor Mindendorfer and some other girls came along the road.

Sue's shrill voice floated across the field to them. "Well, I don't care what you think, Miss Smarty Eleanor," she said. "I just happen to know that — " The rest of her sentence was lost as they walked past.

"Who are those little girls? Are they special friends of yours?" Mrs. North asked, shading her eyes with one hand.

"Oh, they're just some of the dumb kids," Martha said in an offhand way.

" 'Some of the dumb kids!' " Mrs. North turned to look at Martha. "Dumb kids!" she said again. "Why, Martha, that's not a nice way to speak of your little friends."

Martha stared back at Mrs. North, and, because she was embarrassed, she scowled. "I didn't mean anything," she muttered. "I'm sorry."

"I'm glad you didn't mean it, dear," Mrs. North said. Then she added, "Let's walk a little farther, shall we?"

Later they slowly walked back to the school, and Martha told Mrs. North good-bye. Mrs. North was sweet to her and said she was glad to have met her. Martha ducked her head a couple of times, grinned, abruptly shook hands with Mrs. North, and disappeared.

Soon it was time for Mrs. North to leave. She held Victoria close and kissed her. "I miss you so much, Vicky," she whispered. "Someday you won't have to go to boarding school. Someday, darling, we will be together all the time. I promise!" Then the taxi took her away.

Victoria wandered out to the little wood in back of the dormitory. She went to the hut, pulled the door open, and went in and sat down.

It had been wonderful to see her mother again. But her mother hadn't liked the double-decker bed or the swap of the fountain pen for the marbles. And, worst of all, her mother hadn't liked Martha. She hadn't said so. She'd told Victoria that she thought Martha an "interesting little girl." But Victoria could tell she hadn't liked her. It was too bad, because Martha was really the best roommate in the whole world.

Victoria stared out of the three-cornered window of the hut at the pale green leaves of a birch tree. She sighed. She'd looked forward for a long time to her mother's visit, and now it was all over, and she couldn't think of anything else lovely to look forward to. The visit was over, and her mother hadn't liked Martha.

Victoria walked back to the dormitory and went slowly up to their room.

"Hi," Martha said, looking up. She was kneeling by Victoria's bureau. Her voice sounded rather subdued. "You know what, Vicky? We haven't played that Ralmadil boarding-school game in ages. You want to?"

"Oh yes, let's!"

"Help me take the drawer out."

They sat on the floor with the bureau drawer between them. And before the supper gong rang, they took the whole school into the city to luncheon and a matinee.

That night in bed, after lights-out, after the house-mother had told them good night, Martha whispered, "Hey, Vicky. I'm sorry I was a dope in front of your mother."

Victoria was surprised that Martha would say anything so nice. She turned over on her stomach and closed her eyes. "You weren't, Martha," she said. "You weren't a dope. Honest you weren't." After a minute she said, "Good night."

"Good night," Martha said in a whisper.

The Secret Panel

ONE RAINY AFTERNOON Victoria and Martha were reading in their room. But they were both restless, and they wished the rain would stop so they could go out to their hut.

"You know what?" Victoria said, looking up from her book.

"What?"

"I wish we could look around this school and find a secret cubbyhole, or a secret drawer, or something. I've heard of them and I wish we could find one."

Martha closed her book and looked at Victoria with approval. "Well, let's look. Let's start looking," she said.

"How do we look? Do you know?"

"In mystery stories they knock on the walls," Martha said. "If you hit a place that sounds different from the other places, that's a secret compartment. It makes a hollow sound."

She rapped all along one wall with her knuckles.

She climbed up on the top bunk and rapped along that wall and along part of the ceiling.

"Sounds all the same so far," Martha said.

"I'll try in the closet," Victoria said. "That ought to be a good place." She disappeared behind their clothes and began to knock on the walls inside the closet.

When Martha had tested all the walls in the room, she sat down on the floor and knocked on it. But all the spots sounded the same to her. The muffled sound of Victoria's rapping came from the closet. For several minutes both girls worked steadily. They were so intent on their own tapping that neither of them heard a new tap at the door. The tap came again on the door, but still they didn't hear it. Finally the door opened, and the housemother stood in the doorway.

"Why, Martha," she said in amazement. "What on earth are you doing?"

Martha was sitting on the floor, tapping it, with her back to the door. When she heard Miss Denton's voice she turned around quickly, but she could think of nothing to say.

"What are you doing, child?" Miss Denton asked again.

"And what's *that?*" she asked, coming into the room. The tapping from the closet continued, and Martha and the housemother stared at each other in silence. Neither of them moved.

Suddenly Victoria called from inside the closet, "Oh, I give up. I can't find it in here." And she crawled out on hands and knees. Her hair had fallen over her eyes, and her cheeks were pink from the work of tapping.

"Why, hello, Mother Carrie. I didn't know you were here," Victoria said politely, getting to her feet.

"Vicky, what are you girls doing?" the housemother asked faintly. "What couldn't you find in the closet? I heard such strange noises coming from this room. Why was Martha tapping on the floor?"

Victoria glanced at Martha. Then she walked to the door and closed it. "Well, you see," she started, then stopped and looked at Martha for help. But Martha had none to offer. Still seated on the floor, she slowly untied and retied her shoelaces. "Well, you see," Victoria began again, "we just thought we'd like to find a secret compartment someplace, so we started to look in here. But we didn't find one yet."

"A secret compartment?" Miss Denton repeated.

"Yes, you know, or a secret drawer in back of a secret panel, or something."

Miss Denton sat down and put one arm around Victoria, and she laughed and shook her head. "What ever made you decide to do that?" she asked.

Victoria didn't know exactly what to say.

"Well, we need a good old secret drawer," Martha said from the floor. "We need it to put some of our things in. That's all. We'd like to put some important things in a good old secret place."

"I see. Of course." Miss Denton nodded, serious again. "Well, girls, I'm sorry about this, but I can almost promise you that you won't find a secret drawer, panel, or compartment in this building or in this entire school. I'm truly sorry to have to say that, but I think I'm right. This house was built about ten years ago, and people didn't make secret hiding places in houses built so recently. I'm sorry to disappoint you." And, in spite of the fact that she had laughed a moment ago, she did look sorry now.

"Well, what sort of a house would have them?" Martha asked.

"Oh, some old houses in New England, or in the South, probably. Or perhaps a castle in Scotland, or in France."

"But not here in this school?"

"No, dear, not here in this school."

"Oh!" They both looked disappointed.

"But why don't you girls fix up a secret place for yourselves?" Miss Denton asked.

"What do you mean? How?" Martha was puzzled.

"Come, now! You two girls can certainly make your own secret hiding place," Miss Denton said. "You could dig a hole in the floor of your hut. And I have an old strongbox I'll be glad to let you have. It isn't a big box, but it is metal and it has a lock on it, and I think I still have the key to it."

"Oh, leebossa," Martha said. She got up and walked over and stood in front of the housemother. "Oh, leebossa," she said again. "You're nice!"

"Thank you, my dear," said Miss Denton quietly.

"Martha, we can put that strongbox in a good hole and put the dirt back in the hole and cover that place all up, and no one will ever be able to find it." Victoria was excited.

Miss Denton stood up. "Yes, that's the way to do it," she said. "I'm sure it won't rain tomorrow, and you can do it then. I'll get the strongbox now."

At the door she turned back. "Girls, I won't ask you what things you're going to keep in the strongbox," she said. "But you must promise me not to put in it anything your parents have given you. You know what I mean. It is not for watches, or fountain pens, or anything your parents and I would not want you to put in a box in the ground."

"Yes, we know," they said together.

In a few minutes Miss Denton came back with a small but sturdy metal box, and the key.

Into the box they put Victoria's three best marbles, and a blue-gray stone she'd found in the woods. They put in the sea shells Martha had picked up on a beach the summer before, and a beautiful red glass bottle stopper Richy had given Martha, and a long brass chain Martha had found and had given to Victoria.

When everything was in the box, Martha locked it, took the key out of the lock, and said, "Do you want to keep the key?"

"We'll have to hide the key, too," Victoria said slowly.

She took it from Martha and looked at it carefully. Then she smiled. "Oh, Marth! Yes, I'll take it. I just had the most wonderful idea where to keep it!"

"Where?"

"I'll figure it out some more and tell you later," Victoria said. "But it's a good scheme. You'll like it."

"We can put the strongbox in the Ralmadil School drawer until tomorrow," Martha said.

She wandered over to the window and stood looking out at the rain. "Did you hear Miss Denton say she could almost promise us there wouldn't be any secret compartment in this school?" she asked idly.

"Yes, I heard her."

"It's so funny to say 'promise' and then promise something bad. You usually think a promise is going to be something good, don't you?"

"She doesn't, though," Victoria said. "Yesterday she said if I didn't get my arithmetic homework done she'd promise me I wouldn't be promoted. Yes, it's a funny way to talk, all right."

"But she's really not bad," Martha said, turning from the window. "I guess that's just the way she talks."

"I guess so."

They returned to their books.

The next day was sunny. They woke up early and went out to the hut with the strongbox and with two trowels they had borrowed from Mr. Hardy.

They dug a hole, put the strongbox in it, covered it

up with dirt, then scattered pine needles over the spot. The dirt that was left they carried to another part of the woods in a couple of empty cans they'd saved. Then they returned to the hut and stared at the floor.

"No one could tell it was there," Martha said.

"No. No one could."

"Now, what about that big scheme you had about the key, Vick?"

"I haven't quite finished it," Victoria said. "You go on back to the room now, and I'll show you later."

Martha obediently walked away and left Victoria alone.

That afternoon, after classes, they went again to the hut. Victoria handed Martha a folded piece of paper. On it was a rough drawing of the hut with an X at the doorway. Under the drawing Victoria had written:

> Stand at X.
> Take 4 steps forward.
> Then take 2 steps to the left.
> Then take 3 more steps forward.
> Then walk around the tree
> And find our key.

Martha grinned at the directions, read them twice, and said, "Very leebossa."

She followed the directions carefully and found herself beside an apple tree. "This it?"

Victoria nodded happily.

Martha walked around the tree and stared at the ground. Then, with her hands, she started to dig a little hole in the ground at the base of the tree.

"You're cold," Victoria said. "Look for it. You don't have to dig."

Martha looked under some twigs and leaves on the ground, and kicked some stones aside with her foot. Then she looked at Victoria and gave a little shrug. "I guess I give up," she said. "Yes, I give up."

Victoria walked over to the tree, stood on tiptoe, put her right hand up to a crotch in the tree, and took down the strongbox key. She gave it to Martha.

"Hey, that's good!" Martha grinned at the key and then closed her fist over it. "That's a good place to keep it. That was a good scheme."

From then on they kept the key in the crotch of that apple tree, and no one else ever found it.

The Pool

In MAY the soft spring weather came. Lilacs bloomed, and apple blossoms drifted across the ground. On Sundays Victoria and Martha wa..ed to church in their new spring coats, under the blossoming trees. Martha's coat was green, lined with gray silk. Victoria's coat was blue. It was lined with soft blue satin, and its pockets were lined with satin, too. The pockets of her winter coat had been rough to touch, and crammed with the winter's collection of mittens, wads of paper, knotted pieces of string. But the clean, satin-lined pockets of her new spring coat were smooth and fresh to her hands, like the soft, sweet spring.

One sunny day, when Martha and Victoria were sitting beside their hut, leaning against a tree and reading, Mr. Hardy came through the woods toward them.

"Hi," Martha said.

"Good day," said Mr. Hardy. "Just thinking maybe you girls would like to have a little — now I just said *little* — pool in the back of this hut of yours."

"A little pool!" Martha stood up and put a leaf in her book to mark her place before she closed it. "Hey, that's a wonderful idea! But how could we?"

"Well, you'd have to let me fix it for you," Mr. Hardy said flatly. "I can't let you fool around with any cement. But if you want it I can fix you one."

"Thank you very much," Martha said. "We do want one."

"We certainly do," said Victoria.

The next day, when they went to the hut after volley-ball practice, they found Mr. Hardy had finished making the cement-lined pool. It was about two feet in diameter and about six inches deep at the center.

The following day, when the cement was dry, Mr. Hardy brought two pails of water and poured it into the little pool. "There," he said. "That water looks pretty now. But it'll get full of leaves and twigs and green stuff. So every so often you have to scoop it out and clean off that cement and put in clean, fresh water. All right?"

"Oh, we will! Thanks, Mr. Hardy."

"Well, so long," Mr. Hardy said. "You keep that pool clean, now." And he walked away with his pails.

"He's nice," Victoria said. She and Martha lay on their stomachs and looked at their reflections in the water.

"I guess before this term is over we should ask Miss Denton to come see our hut," Martha said, staring into the pool.

That was what Victoria had been wanting to do. "Yes, let's!" she said.

When the housemother came in after lights-out, Martha said, "Vicky and I want you to come see our hut."

"I'd love to, dear. Tomorrow I have to attend a faculty meeting, but I could come the next day. That's Thursday."

"All right. Right after volleyball we'll come back here for you. Don't forget, now."

"I won't. Good night, girls."

After she'd left, Victoria waited a few minutes, then whispered, "Martha, you asleep?"

"No."

"You know what?"

"No, what?"

"You like Mother Carrie now."

Martha didn't answer.

"You do, too. You didn't for awhile, but you do now."

"Oh, she's all right," Martha said. Then she added, "Yes, I like her."

The next day Victoria suggested that they make the housemother a May basket, even though it was after May Day.

"All right," Martha said. "I bet she would like it."

They got up early the next morning and took the cover off a wicker sewing basket Martha's Aunt Nellie had given her. They emptied the basket and took it out to the woods behind the hut.

They lined the basket with moss, and Martha sprinkled it with water from their pool, so it would stay damp and fresh. They found some violets and stuck them into the moss. Victoria broke a small twig off a maple tree. There were two pale little green leaves on the twig, and when they put it firmly in the bed of moss it looked like a miniature tree. Martha added a small sprig of lilac, and the basket began to look beautiful. The flowers seemed to be growing right out of the moss.

"Hey, Vicky," Martha said, "I'll go get that little round mirror I saved from my mother's old evening bag she threw away. We can put that in to look like a little pool!"

"Oh, that's a wonderful idea. But do you think it will look like a little pool?"

They tried it, and it did.

Then the May basket was finished, and they put it in the shade inside the hut, so it would stay fresh.

"Mother Carrie, this is our lovely hut," Victoria said when she and Martha and the housemother stood before it.

"It is a very lovely and interesting hut, girls," the housemother said. "My gracious, I never dreamed you two girls had built such a fine hut."

"Oh, we can make an even better one next year," Martha said. "Now the surprise, Vick. You wait there a minute, Miss Denton."

Both girls went into the hut, and in a moment they called out, "Now close your eyes!"

They came out with the May basket and walked over to the housemother and held it in front of her.

"All right. Now open your eyes," Martha said.

"Why, that is the loveliest May basket I have ever seen," Miss Denton said. "And the mirror pool looks just like your pool! Oh, thank you, girls."

All three looked at the May basket in silence. "It is truly beautiful," the housemother said at last. Then she looked over at their own pool.

"You know, girls," she said, "you could plant lilies of the valley beside your pool. And they would bloom beside it next spring, and the spring after that, and the spring after that, and every spring for years and years to come."

"They would? For years and years?" asked Victoria.

"Yes. Lily of the valley blooms every year, year after year after year."

"But we won't be here," Victoria said blankly. "In years and years we won't be here!"

"No, you won't be here years and years from now," the housemother admitted. "But other children will be here then, and maybe they'll find the pool, and if they do, the lilies of the valley you plant will be here for them."

"Hey, maybe we wouldn't like those kids," Martha

said. "I don't want to plant any flowers for any dumb
kids to find. We might not like them."

"No, but then again you might. In fact, two of them
might be just like you two girls," the housemother said
slowly.

"Just like us!" Victoria exclaimed in amazement.
"How could they be like us?"

"Well, perhaps not, dear. Perhaps they wouldn't be."
The housemother smiled at her. "Well, thank you both
for my lovely May basket. I do think it is beautiful, and
I think your hut is, too. I'll see you at supper."

She walked away, holding her May basket carefully.
The girls sat down beside the pool.

"Marth, you said we could build a better hut next
year," Victoria said. "You are going to come back, aren't
you, Marth? Aren't you?"

"No. No, I'm not. Not unless they make me," Martha
replied slowly. But she sounded less certain than she
ever sounded before.

"Come In and
Put Your Sweaters On"

THE LOVELY DAYS grew longer. On sunny days Miss
Denton allowed the girls on her corridor to stay out-
doors until seven-thirty. Most of them went down to the
swings after supper. But that was the time of day when
Martha and Victoria liked to sit on the stone steps of
Wingate Hall and play jacks in the late May sunshine.

"It's so hot we don't have to wear our sweaters, do
we?" Martha asked.

"Well," the housemother said, "when it is really sunny
you don't have to put them on until seven o'clock. But
it does get chilly by then. So at seven you must come in
and put your sweaters on, Martha. But then you can go
out again and play until seven-thirty."

Victoria loved Mother Carrie. And by that time Martha loved the housemother, too, though as yet she would
not admit it. Nevertheless, neither of the girls ever remembered to go indoors for their sweaters when the
school-hall clock struck seven. Evening after evening
the housemother had to come out to remind them that

118

it was time for them to come in and put their sweaters on. She was always patient and kind, but she seemed increasingly sad that they never did as she had asked them to do. Every evening she would come out and say, "Girls, you promised me that if I let you play outdoors without your sweaters, you would come in and put them on at seven o'clock." She would look up at the school-hall clock and shake her head. "It is seven-fifteen and again you make it necessary for me to come out here to remind you. That's not thoughtful, girls. Now come in and put your sweaters on."

One evening they were playing jacks on the steps as usual. Martha was up to fivesies. All of a sudden she looked up at the clock, which was just beginning to strike seven. Martha finished fivesies and started on sixsies.

"About time for Miss Denton to come out and tell us to come in and put our sweaters on," she remarked.

"Yes, it is," Victoria said. "Martha, you know what?"

"No, what?"

"Why don't we go in and put our sweaters on now?"

"Why Vicky, that's a wonderful idea!" Martha said. "That's wonderful. Let's! She'll be happy."

"All right, then?" Victoria looked at her.

"Oh, yes, let's!" Martha said. She was pleased with Victoria's suggestion. "Then she won't have to come out here and tell us to come in and put our sweaters on."

And at that precise moment the door opened and Miss

Denton said sadly, "Once more you girls make it necessary for me to tell you to come in and put your sweaters on."

"Oh!" Victoria howled, and she got to her feet. She couldn't bear it. "Oh! We were *just* — " She stopped and stared at Martha.

Martha had hurled herself at the housemother and clutched her awkwardly around the waist. "We were!" Martha wailed. She was actually crying. "Honest! Honest we were! We were just coming in to put our old sweaters on. Honest, Mother Carrie!"

The housemother did not show that she had noticed that Martha had finally called her Mother Carrie. She just said briskly, "There now, Martha. I'm glad to know you were about to come in and put your sweaters on." She patted Martha's shoulder. "Now, hurry, girls. You can stay out for almost another half-hour if you hurry for your sweaters."

By that time Martha had collected herself and wiped the tears away with the back of her hand, and she and Victoria went upstairs to put their sweaters on.

They both called the housemother Mother Carrie from then on, and it was a great relief to Victoria. It was a great relief to Martha, too.

"Then We
Go to the Station"

As the end of the school year grew closer, the rhythm of life at Coburn School seemed to quicken every day. Autograph books were passed around and home addresses were exchanged. Everyone talked about final examinations and summer vacation. It stayed light until almost nine o'clock, and after supper many of the older boys and girls, and a few of the younger ones, walked around the track together.

One evening, when Victoria was playing hopscotch with Martha and Sue Burton, Peter Fay, who was in the fifth grade, came over to her.

"Hey, Vicky," he said. "Want to walk around the track?"

Victoria looked at him in amazement. "Who, me?" she said.

"Yes, you. Want to walk around the track?" he repeated.

Victoria looked away in embarrassment. "Well, I can't right now," she said. "I'm busy. But thank you for asking me."

As Peter walked away, Sue giggled, and Martha said, "Hey, Peter Fay likes you. You know it?"

"Oh, Martha," Victoria protested. "He does not."

"He does, too," Martha repeated. She sounded puzzled.

"I've never even spoken to him in my whole born life!"

"Well, he likes you, all right," Martha said.

"Oh, ick-en-spick," said Victoria, in confusion.

The days flew by. Final examinations were given, and Martha and Victoria passed all subjects. And then the day came when Mr. Hardy brought the children's trunks up to their rooms to be packed and sent home before the school closed.

Mother Carrie went from room to room to supervise and to help. She found Victoria sitting inside her large, square trunk. "Hello, Mother Carrie," Victoria said happily. "This trunk is my lovely boat and I'm going to sail it home."

"Vicky North, you land that boat at once and step ashore," the housemother said. She sat down and took a pencil and paper out of her pocket. "Well, girls," she said. "Glad to be going home at last?"

"Yes," said Martha.

"You know what, though?" Victoria said, getting out of her trunk.

"What, dear?"

"We'll miss you."

"Thank you, dear. I'll certainly miss you girls. You know, you've both changed a great deal," the housemother said thoughtfully. "You've both grown up quite a bit this year. Do you feel you have?"

"Well, I guess everybody is more grown up now than they were," Martha said reasonably.

"No, not everybody," Mother Carrie said. "Tell me, do you girls think you have learned things this year? I don't mean in school work, necessarily."

Martha and Victoria exchanged glances. They never enjoyed the little talks the housemother liked to have with them from time to time. Because they loved Mother Carrie, they tried to be interested in anything she wanted to discuss. But usually they didn't know what to say.

"Well, I learned how to make a bed," Victoria offered. She wondered if that was the sort of thing Mother Carrie had in mind.

"Anything else?"

"I learned the secret language," Victoria said.

"I wonder if you know that I've never approved of that secret language," the housemother said. "I haven't said anything about it before because I suppose it is natural for girls your age to want to have secrets. But as you grow up you'll realize, I hope, that it is not thoughtful to say things others cannot understand."

"Well, if other people don't like it they can make up their own secret language if they want to — and not tell us," Martha said.

"Rather unfortunately, none of the other children did that this year," Mother Carrie remarked dryly. "If they had, I am sure you would have found it most unpleasant."

"Well, what else have I learned?" Victoria said, half to herself.

Martha began to grin. "I learned that a midnight feast is no fun," she said.

"I learned not to be homesick," Victoria said.

"And that's a great deal, dear," Mother Carrie said, getting up and going to the door. "I really think you both learned a great deal this year. But we won't talk about it any more now. I'll come back later to help you pack."

After Mother Carrie left, Martha sat down on her bed. "You know what? I wanted to tell her I learned some housemothers are nicer than some other housemothers," she said. "But she'd have thought she had to say something to stick up for that old Miss Mossman."

"Yes, she would have," Victoria agreed. "She always thinks she has to stick up for everybody," she added regretfully. "But she's nice."

"Yes, she sure is," said Martha.

That night in bed Victoria began to whisper first. "Martha, aren't you really coming back next year?"

Martha was silent.

Victoria leaned over the side of her bed and looked down at Martha in the faint moonlight. "Aren't you, Marth? When we showed Mother Carrie the hut, you did say we could build a better one next year. You said it right out. You are coming back, aren't you?"

Martha got out of bed and went over to the window. She leaned on the window sill and looked up at the moonlit sky. "I don't know," she said finally. "I just don't know, Vicky. But probably they'll make me."

"I'll have to come back. And if you come back too, we could have fun, Martha. We could build a better hut, and we could think up a good idea for the Halloween Party, and maybe we could start to work out some thought transference with each other. And we could try to do some mind reading on the teachers. I bet we could have fun, Marth."

Martha got back into bed. "Maybe we could," she said. "Well, I'll probably have to come back. And if I do, we'll room together. All right?"

"Oh, yes," whispered Victoria.

And then they both fell asleep.

The day school closed, the children left in two separate groups. The first group went in the morning, the second late in the afternoon.

Martha left in the morning. Victoria, who was to leave with the second group, waved good-bye to her and then went back to their room alone. The room looked strange. The beds were stripped bare, and the closet was empty except for the coat and hat Victoria was to wear home. She wandered downstairs and found Mother Carrie in the drawing room.

"Hello, dear," the housemother said. "Are you excited?"

"Yes."

"Well, I know you and your mother will have a lovely summer, and we'll see each other in the fall, won't we?"

"Yes," Victoria said. "Oh, I hope Martha will come back!"

"Maybe she will, dear," Mother Carrie said. "She might, you know."

"But it will be awful if she doesn't!"

"Now, Vicky," Mother Carrie said. "Even if she doesn't come back, you'll be all right. You mustn't forget that next year you'll be one of the old girls."

"Yes, I will be, won't I!" The thought surprised and pleased Victoria.

"You certainly will be. There's the luncheon gong. Let's go to the dining room together, shall we, this last time?"

Later in the afternoon Victoria and the others who were to leave next waited in front of Wingate Hall. Mother Carrie and Mrs. Coburn and a few children who were not leaving until the next day came out to see them off.

"Be good on the train," Mother Carrie said. "Be thoughtful of Miss Douglass, won't you? Now, here's the bus. Good-bye, girls!"

"Good-bye!"

"Good-bye, Mother Carrie!"

"Good-bye!"

Victoria sat at the back of the bus, and when the driver started the engine, she knelt on the back seat and stared out the window. The old bus rattled on to the station. And as Victoria looked back, the buildings of the school and the few grownups and children still left there slowly became smaller and smaller. And then the school gradually disappeared in the distance, and finally it was hidden from her sight by the green trees and the hills.